"Bone Diggers"

By Michael James

Copyright 2012

Print Edition

This is a work of fiction. The names, characters, places and incidents in this writing are either products of the author's imagination or used fictitiously. Any resemblance to actual events, locales, or persons living or dead is entirely coincidental.

No part of this publication can be reproduced or transmitted by any means electronic or mechanical without express permission in writing of its author. Doing so is illegal and punishable by law.

Contact the author at: https://www.facebook.com/mjssouthwriter?ref=hl

Or: Michaelj1492@live.com

This book is dedicated to Native people everywhere. I would like to thank my family who patiently put up with me through the long nights and the very early mornings while I wrote this. Special thanks to my dogs that were forever by my side. I would like to thank my friends at the Seminole Tribune and others who patiently answered some tough questions over and over again. I would like to thank the Florida State Archives and the Florida Museum of History, Ah-Tah-Thi-Ki Museum, The Canadian Museum of Civilization, Alan from the Smithsonian Institute, Dr. Robin Brown, and Arden for your time and boat gas. Special thanks to Tracy Pope Phillips and Toni Bennett Doyle for your energy and help with the relentless editing.

Prologue

It's not the things that you see and know that are scary. It's the things that remain hidden. Things that are in the ground or the air and in the dark. If we are fortunate enough to spend seventy years here we can condition ourselves with the unique human tool of logic and tell ourselves that everything will be okay. If we look back and try to see where we came from, things begin to get a little muddy and a little scarier once we realize that on the big timeline, we aren't too far removed from witches, monsters, and unexplained things that go bump in the night. We can know some of these things from what is left behind but for as long as humans have put other humans in the ground, mummified them, preserved them, and ceremoniously and reverently sent them on their way to the afterlife or eternal rest, there have always been others willing to disrupt that rest. Grave robbers and privateers are everywhere, they always have been. Maybe even in your own backyard.

Table of contents

Chapter 1

There is no modern language construct to give him a name. Jesus had come and gone a thousand years ago and neither knew anything about the other. His people didn't write but surely he had a name. Surely he loved, hurt, wondered, dreamt, knew fear, and pride as well. He was tall and handsome and brave and would soon take a wife. He had spent the last five years going out with the men who made up the hunting parties, the same men that made up the war parties from the village although he never went to war. Those skills would come later. During the last two years of his transition to manhood he mastered crafts that would keep him and his loved ones alive. It took him nearly two years of constant work and practice to learn how to prepare pieces of chert and work them into useful tools like spear points, knives, and arrow heads. Even before that, long before he would ever be able to go with the men he sat with a piece of leather across his thigh and another one in his hand like he had seen the adults do. He chipped and banged and broke hundreds of pieces of stone into extremely sharp chips and flakes while the women made the finest pots out of clay that came from the river two days travel away and to the northwest. He would sit in his place amongst them, with his right foot drawn back under his left thigh. He would work on the stone pieces so long that when he rose, there would be a pattern of chips all around so that you could see where he sat. Sometimes he would cut his hands and fingers and he bore the scars of thousands of attempts to create something useful.

He would always sit in the same place so he wouldn't lacerate himself by sitting in a pile of the razor sharp flakes.

His masterpiece was a four inch long knife blade made from agatized coral that he had affixed to a carved handle made from gumbo limbo wood. His grandfather has traded for both the wood and the stone from the water people he heard his grandfather speak of from far away, even further than where the clay came from. He made a scabbard out of deer hide and adorned it with rattlesnake skin that he carefully stitched together with the fibers of the yucca. He wore his creation on a belt made for him by his aunt and mother.

Now he was ready. For several months he had worked and carefully crafted a fine bow of hickory wood that was so strong that few in the village could pull it back. No one else really needed to pull it back because it was his; it was made to fit him. He spent hours carefully shaving off miniscule layers of wood in shavings sometimes only a few cells thick, then he would restring the bow, pull it, flex it, unstring it again, adjust it some more until it became an extension of him. He could shoot the head off of a duck sized bird at forty paces. His quiver contained four long arrows each tipped with a chert point not much bigger than a thumbnail. The tiny and light tips sped through the air, their flight controlled by turkey feather fletching on the back of them. The fletching had been carefully applied, gently glued down with boiled pine tar that made a sticky glue and then wound down tightly with fine plant fibers. The arrows didn't kill by brute force or speed but rather by the elegant and humane method of massive hemorrhage and deadly accuracy. There were other arrows in his quiver as well. Two were tipped with stingray barbs and he used those to take fish, and two more were tipped with small blunt stones. Though not as fast a rifle bullet, the blunt tips contained nearly as much energy as some modern rifle rounds and they were very efficient for taking small game. He had mastered the bow and the atlatl and would someday be one of the most skilled hunters in the camp.

His village was south of what is known today as Lake Okeechobee. It was situated in a live oak hammock next to an expansive marsh. The marsh was fed from a large creek that provided a transportation route for the people. The village site had been built up over hundreds of years by many hands adding baskets of soil from the surrounding area. During the highest water of the wettest season, the village was at least two feet higher than the ground it was built on. Food was plentiful in and along the marsh. There were many birds, turtles, fish, eggs, and plants that were good to eat. Big game could be found in the deep woods to the west.

On this day he found himself far from the village and alone. He had carefully and quietly stalked a woodland bison for many miles without the animal ever knowing of his presence. It was late in the afternoon when he finally closed the distance enough to take a shot at the giant animal. He knew his success would be better if he could launch one of his atlatl darts through the rib cage of the beast but felt like he was just a little bit out of range for the dart. He continued his stalk moving ever so slowly toward the animal and each time he did the bison would graze on ahead a little way with his rump facing him. Finally the bison turned fully around as if he heard or smelled something. He had his chest squared to the hunter when the arrow flew. Just as the arrow released the archer heard the characteristic buzz of a rattlesnake and he flinched slightly. The arrow penetrated the chest and deflected downward missing the heart, the aorta, and just about everything else vital. It did nick a lung before it moved on through and then exiting the belly of the bison. The animal gave a loud bellow to signal its displeasure and trotted off into the deep woods.

The hunter killed the snake, collected himself and went off in the last known direction of the bison. He followed the trail and the very few drops of blood until it got dark. He spent the night in the woods in the dark, not wanting to draw attention to where he was and he didn't want to frighten the great beast that he had wounded.

At first light he continued his hunt. He was relentless in his pursuit and finally about two hours before it would be dark again he found the bison dead, lying in a dark hammock of oak trees with a shaft of light illuminating him.

He approached him cautiously from behind. When he closed the distance to the animal by half, the first spear struck him in his shoulder and was quickly followed by another that struck him at the base of his skull nearly severing his head. He had followed the bison far and into the territory of the fierce people that he heard his elders speak of before. They had no anger with the young man, no malice. They simply killed other people that they found in what they considered their territory, especially people who hunted there. Whether by design or by accident it didn't matter, interlopers were all treated the same. It was an innate protective function of their culture as much as it was a political statement.

The four fierce hunter/warriors trussed the young brave up on a pole like they would have a deer or other game and they set out for his home territory. They kept his bow and his knife as spoils and they carried his body through the night chanting in a cadence that they kept pace to. Once they could see the fires from the village, they hefted the pole and the young man off their shoulders, retrieved the thongs that had bound him and returned to where they came from.

By mid-day the next afternoon, some of the people in the village had noticed the vultures circling in the sky close to the horizon. A party of men was dispatched to go see what the commotion in the sky was all about. When they arrived at site they were horrified by their discovery of the young man's body and they began to wail. One of the men reached into a pouch and withdrew a small round bundle which he ignited with a smoldering coal that he carried with him. He walked around the corpse with the smoking bundle until he made a full circle around it. The village men fixed a truss similar to the one the killers had used and they brought the body back to the village. Special wood and leaves were put on the fire to burn and once everyone had seen him and paid their respects the medicine man came for him. He cut two very generous amounts of hair from the head of the body and divided it between the woman who was to bear his children, immediate female family members, and the two oldest people in his clan. Everyone was quiet as the men hoisted the pole the body was tied to back up on their shoulders and departed off the side of the village mound down to the marsh and out of sight.

There was a hut at the top of the low burial mound where the medicine man lived and conducted his work. The top of the mound was scarcely two feet above the surrounding muck and any hoe dug into it quickly filled with water. He didn't associate with the people of the village because of the nature of his work and he frightened the children. The medicine man went up the side of the mound into the hut and returned with a mat of woven palm fronds. The men lowered the body onto the mat that was supported by poles and then helped the medicine man situate it inside the hut. They gathered a large amount of fire wood for the man. They were given instructions by the medicine man to retrieve certain personal articles that belonged to the young man, when to bring them back, and he sent them back to the village. After some distance they looked back even though they were instructed not to and they could see a large fire burning with the man moving around it, as he moved he also turned in small circles.

After the sun went down the medicine man built a small fire in a large ceramic bowl and he moved it into the house. It provided light and enough smoke to keep the bugs away. Once his eyes adjusted he went to work. Since the head was mostly severed from the attack it was easy to remove. He carefully skinned it and removed most of the contents of the skull. The rest of the body was gently skinned much like a deer would be. The bones were all disarticulated and scraped clean with the help of several different chert knives. The skin was put in a bag made of deerskin and filled with water and wood ashes. The bones went into another bag full of water and both of them were hung by the rafters of the hut. What remained was taken down to the edge of the marsh and dumped by the water.

The old medicine man was tired now. He stoked the fire pot with more fuel and added different leaves and the bark of medicinal trees he then laid down and slept under the bags hanging from the rafter poles.

The preparation went on for nearly a month. The bones had been boiled free of any remaining tissue and had been bleached white in the relentless sun. The skin had been tanned and stretched and then softened over many hours. When the process was complete he arranged the bones in the skin in an order that only he knew and stitched it closed. He then wrapped the bundle in another finely crafted palm leaf mat and tied it off. At the appointed time the others returned to the charnel house bearing the items they were instructed to bring. The skin bundle was rolled up in a grass mat and tied off again. The female relatives of the slain each brought two ceramic pots. One had the bottom knocked out if it, the other remained intact. Men brought a few beads, some feathers, and a couple of spear points. The medicine man had a hole prepared near the top of the mound and off to one side. He placed the bundle in the hole along with the grave goods and with each item muttered a quiet chant. When the hole was filled the people returned to the village leaving the medicine man behind to do his bidding. Tonight very powerful spirits would gather around the burial and hopefully take another back with them.

Chapter 2

The second annual meeting of the Florida Treasure Hunters and Cultural Preservation Society had convened in Tallahassee for their winter event. They were there in part to protest laws governing the collection of artifacts of any description from public or private lands. Surface collecting on private land had been considered within the bounds of the law as it stood but now because of increased pressure from the tribes across the country, that practice was called into question and was likely going to be banned during this session. Several hundred members of the Society had shown up in motor homes, minivans, cars, pickup trucks, motorcycles and other forms of conveyance. They camped, stayed in cheap motels along the Parkway, some even parked their Winnebagos in the parking decks reserved for state employees. The campers staked out their territory with rebel flags, homemade flags about state's rights, and there was even a jolly roger or two seen flapping in the balmy gulf breeze. By day they would go to the meetings and present poorly constructed arguments about why it should be legal to pick up artifacts that nobody cared about. Things have just laid there for a thousand years, things that had been stepped over, plowed under, and just left out there to rot. It was only fair that if they were going to go to all the trouble to research these finds they should be able to keep them. Most of them actually thought they were helping the professional archaeologists employed by the state. When they weren't in meetings they were out all over town and in school yards with their high priced metal detectors. They loved their metal detectors and loved to talk about them and what that had found with them. They would spread out all over the place between meetings and in the late afternoon. They looked like a paramilitary organization sweeping for land mines. The city officials were constantly throwing them off historic property both public and private. They would comb across vast areas with headphones, green army surplus shoulder bags, folding shovels, and garden trowels and at night they would sit together and show off what they had found.

The finder's keeper's argument was a good argument, at least to Jimmy Goodland. He was the self-proclaimed leader of the society who had somehow gained audience with the legislative body who listened sometimes for hours to his pseudo-scientific litany about how people just like him are responsible for 'saving' the cultural heritage of ancient Floridians. Jimmy knew lots of people and he was a master name dropper. He could rattle off the names of artists, PhD level archaeologists, prominent Indians, historical characters, city and county managers and other notorious Floridians for hours. For many of the newly installed Florida politicos it sounded convincing enough. Most of them came from somewhere else anyway and their biggest concern was following protocol. That was the ticket to the pot of gold at the end of the Florida political rainbow. What if Jimmy did know these people? Some of the names were those of hugely influential people, people that needed political favors and people who would handsomely reward those who granted those favors. It was the elected Florida official retirement system, the underbelly reason why transplants from the Midwest and the northeast get into Florida politics in the first place. Jimmy knew this and if all the names he dropped turned out to be nothing more than a load of gator shit it didn't matter because the people he was trying to sell his story to didn't know the difference.

By day Jimmy argued that if he was at the beach and picked up a shell that was his business but if he picked up that same shell on an Indian Mound in downtown Bradenton he could get a big fine or even jail time.

"How does anyone know the difference? What does it matter? Who cares if it lies around in the sun for the next thousand years or if I pick it up and trade it to one of the members of the Society?"

Over and over he would get the same answer. It was not that anyone really cared that he picked up a piece of shell, a shard of pottery, or a broken stone point. What matters is that the items belonged to all the people of the state, not the least of which included the Native Americans living there. No one had a right whether perceived or implied, to gather items of cultural heritage for their own use. There were dozens of people employed by the state that had the education and the means to interpret a site without the help of a backyard Indiana Jones. Jimmy didn't see it that way and he rebutted everything that contradicted him with another argument, none of which held water.

By night he was the antithesis of what he

preached by day. Society people that had come to the capitol would show up at Jimmy's motor home at dark. He usually had lots of things cooking on the grill and he welcomed everyone. If nothing else it was a cheap place for the members to eat. Once Jimmy's liquor and beer started flowing, tongues would loosen and artifacts would begin to make their way around the fire circle.

A couple from Lake City brought out a display of spear points that they claimed came from a village site near Manatee Springs and they told an elaborate story of how they came to be in possession of them. They talked with Jimmy for a few minutes, had another drink and in no time Jimmy shook the man's hand, rolled up the canvas bag that held the points and put them inside his motor home.

He had paid the equivalent of a couple of barbecued ribs, a few shots of cheap whiskey, and fifty dollars for items that were priceless.

Late that night after the amateurs had gone back to their beds a couple of hard core antiquities 'experts' stayed on. They were tried and true friends of Benny's.

Junior Davis was a big man. Junior was in his mid-fifties but fit as a commando. He wore a dirty gray felt cowboy hat that was pulled down in the front to either shade his eyes or hide them. He wore western style shirts with the sleeves cut off of them all the time. In the winter he word a sleeveless vest stuffed with some sort of waterproof material and when it was cold outside he loved to tell everyone how warm he was in his vest. He sold used cars at a dealership in Ft. Myers but his passion was 'arkeelogy' but he preferred to be called a collector of antiquities. He was much smarter than he looked or sounded which proved to be valuable to him on many occasions. His favorite thing in the world was playing dumb from some out of town 'collector' with more money than brains. Once he hooked one of those characters he played him like a fish, sometimes for months. He would build the buyer up with photos, wild claims and fake documents. When the time was right he would arrange for a deposit in the form of a money order. Once he had the deposit he would set up a meeting with the buyer at some out of the way dumpy motel then he would liberate the buyer of a lot more money in exchange for a handful of junk, then he would disappear. Most of the time the buyer would never know the difference. They would shake his hand, thank him, see him to the door and smile the entire time.

The one person he would never cheat or even think about cheating was Jimmy Goodland. Jimmy was a cunning businessman. He was also ruthless. Jimmy never took kindly to being ripped off and Junior respected that. Junior had seen firsthand what happened to a guy one night that had tried to put one over on old Jimmy. Jimmy had met the man at a little bar in Pass A Grille to make a deal on some spear points and a pot that supposedly came from somewhere in the Kissimmee Valley. He was an expert at his trade and he could pick out a fake form a mile away. Jimmy knew right away that they were fakes, a modern attempt to make something out of nothing. He went along with the ruse and acted excited. Jimmy was so excited that he didn't want to trade any cash around in front of the many strangers so they left the bar and headed south. Somewhere about mid-way along the old Skyway Bridge, Jimmy punched the man in the face so hard that his world went dark. It scared Junior who was sitting in the back seat. Jimmy then walked the man out to the guard rail and sat him down on it. He lectured him for a while about trying to rip him off, then tied a forty pound block around his left ankle and gently pushed him over the edge into the swirling outgoing tide.

Jimmy had known Junior since Junior was a kid, he knew his dad, his mother and his grandparents too. He had also been in the same place that Junior was at in his career and he knew the ropes. He liked Junior and he trusted him. He liked him because if nothing else, Junior was a relentless grave robber that would stop at nothing. He had a reputation among the few that knew him of boring holes through village sites and ancient burials all over Florida, Georgia, and Alabama. He let nothing get in his way. He could live in a tent or out of the back of his pickup for weeks on end. If things got too uncomfortable with the authorities he would simply pack up and move to the next site until things calmed down. He researched law enforcement and knew who most of the people were that were trying to put a stop to his activity. He knew to the point of where they lived and who their friends were. Junior was a master at evasion. Junior was smart but he relied on

Jimmy for two things. He needed Jimmy's sixth sense and ability to research historical records. Junior didn't read too well and he never had the patience to sit in a library or browse historical archives on the computer. More importantly though, he needed Jimmy to liquidate the spoils. Junior had spent three years in the state prison for his fifth arrest trying to sell items of cultural significance and identity. The last time he got caught was at a flea market and this was the final straw that sent him away. He was scared now or at least overly cautious even though he had been out of jail for nearly four years.

Jimmy on the other hand didn't travel in the same circles as the flea market crowd even though they were the main constituents of the Florida Treasure Hunters and Cultural Preservation Society. He used them and most of them were too dumb to realize it. Jimmy had developed a unique following of collectors over his forty year career in the business. Their numbers were few, maybe a dozen all total but they were powerful and had the money to spend. Rumor had it that there were a couple of dentists, a plastic surgeon, several investment bankers, a museum curator, a judge, and possibly several powerful politicians with very tight connections within the Division of State Heritage and Antiquities itself including at least one prominent archaeologist. Jimmy didn't peddle junk. He certainly didn't deal with people who would put him at risk. His clientele was untouchable as far as he could tell. Jimmy and his clients had mutual respect for each other because they both knew that either party could land the other in prison for a very long time if something went wrong. The last thing either side wanted was a hundred armed agents from the Department if the Interior or the State blasting a door down on Key Biscayne and storming a home looking for artifacts.

After a couple of shots of whiskey and long after the others had left for the night Jimmy spoke.

"Whatcha' got for me Junior?"

A broad smile spread across Junior's face, even in the low light from the Chinese lantern hanging around the awning Jimmy could tell he was smiling.

"Got a couple of things you might be interested in," said Junior.

"Bring it over, let's see what you got," said Jimmy.

"Jimmy, we may want to go inside for this," said Junior.

"Hot damn, then let's just go inside," said Jimmy as he rose from his folding chair. He clapped his hands together once and then rubbed them together in a subtle signal that he was in a hurry to see what Junior had brought to the table this time.

Junior pushed back his hat and moved up to the folding table that doubled by night as a bed. There was a retractable light with a shade on it hanging over the table. Jimmy by that point had pulled a barstool up to the table across from Junior. A lit cigarette hung from his dry lips. He took it out of his mouth so he could slug down a little more of his signature drink, vodka and Mountain Dew. He liked to call the concoction a

'Mountain Driver'.

"Show me whatcha' got," said Jimmy.

Junior produced two velvet Crown Royal sacks and a box about the size of a cigar box that he had lined with foam rubber and velvet. He turned the first sack over and emptied it on the soft pad that Bobby had put there for just such a time. He tipped the sack and pulled it across the pad. One by one the items dropped out and away from the leading edge of the sack.

The first item out was a chert knife blade. Jimmy picked it up and turned it in his hand. He raised it up to the light. The edge of it was so fine that the light from the fixture shone through the edge of it in a warm tone of orange. There were no chips in it, no damage, it was perfect, a good sign that this piece had never been handled since it was made. It certainly had never been traded.

The second item was another knife blade in equally good condition. The last two items that came out of the sack were spear points. They were perfect too. Jimmy was already running the dollars through his head as he mentally identified the perfect client who would purchase them from him.

The next bag contained several dozen finely crafted arrow heads. Jimmy described them as bird points but in actuality they were intended for warm blooded targets of substantial size, even human sized targets. They were perfect and undoubtedly came from a cache that someone had created. They were stored somewhere in the event they would be needed. Perhaps along a game trail, an ambush point, somewhere significant where many arrow heads would be handy in the event they were needed quickly.

"These are perfect," said Jimmy. "None of them have ever been used, they are absolutely perfect."

"I thought you might like those," said Junior as he raised the cigar box up to the table. He adjusted the light down closer to the box. He turned the box so that when he opened it the lid would move back away from Jimmy in a dramatic presentation. Jimmy looked intently at the box as Junior reached over it with his fingers and gently lifted it open. There were five indentations in the dark blue velvet, each with an individual treasure tucked into it. Jimmy's attention went immediately to a human vertebra with a broken off spear point imbedded in it. The bone was pure white. The point was broken off flush with the surface of the bone. He picked it up gently and rotated it in the light. On the underside of it, the tip of the point protruded slightly past the bone surface.

"A killing shot wouldn't you say?" said Jimmy. He thought to himself that historically, kill shots commanded premium prices and he knew that with this one item he could potentially quit work for a year or two, maybe forever.

"That's a kill shot my friend," said Junior. "No doubt about it. If that sucker weren't dead before this hit him he certainly was shortly afterwards."

Jimmy got up from the table and hurried over to a cabinet in the kitchen area that was held closed by cheap plastic clip whenever the motor home was traveling. He flipped on the scrawny twelve volt light and retrieved a twenty five year old anatomy book that he picked up at a flea market a couple of years ago. He brought it back over to the table and thumbed through it until he got to the section on skeletons. He carefully picked through the images while he glanced at the bone with the spear point lodged in it. He started at the base of the spine and carefully reviewed the normal dimensions of each bone in the book. Finally after reviewing each bone and after measuring the one in the box he exclaimed, "This dude was shot in the neck."

"Let me see," said Junior.

"Look, see the way this bone has this little curved out place? This is where it sat on top of the one below it. See these fins? They are small. They are the exact size they should be for the second vertebra down from the base of the skull."

"He got shot from behind. That sucks, probably never saw it coming."

"No shit. He never knew it. He was being hunted and when the time came, when the moment was right, someone launched this point through his spine," said Jimmy. "He dropped like a rock."

"Wonder whut happened next?" asked Junior. Think they ate him?"

Junior, don't be a dumb ass. People here didn't each one another. No need to, they had plenty of grub everywhere, it's not like they were hungry," said Jimmy.

"Yeah but in other places in the world some people would eat their enemies just to get even or get their power," said Junior.

"There is no evidence of anyone here ever eating anybody else," said Jimmy. Junior just looked at him and smiled.

Jimmy looked at the other items and the only other impressive object in the box was a six inch long piece of leg bone from a deer or some other similar sized animal that had cut marks on it. The marks were made with stone tools when it was butchered. The unique thing about this piece was that it was intact. Usually long bones were broken open in order to get to the nutritious marrow. This one was not. Maybe the hunters had been ambushed by a predator or other people and they had to stop what they were doing in a hurry. That was left up to conjecture as so many questions usually were when it came to ancient artifacts and remains. As Jimmy closed up the box Junior reached into his pocket for one last item. He withdrew his hand and opened it slowly under the light to reveal a gleaming silver piece of eight that was slightly larger than a modern quarter. Jimmy's eyes lit up. He knew what it was immediately. He took the coin and rolled it around in his hand as he moved his fingers over the relief. He took a jewelers loupe out of his shirt pocket even though he really didn't need to inspect it that closely to realize its significance. He could easily read that is was minted in 1736. The coins were used in the early American colonies well until the mid 1700's, and this was the question. Was it part of a shipwreck or was it one of the thousands of coins used in Colonial America? If it was the later then it was no big deal. If it came from a shipwreck then there would be more where this one came from. Not just pieces of eight either, there could be gold, lots of it, emeralds, jewelry, tools and cannons as well. Now there were many questions that had Jimmy's interest piqued. His mind raced through his list of clients. If there were more items, gold, who would he approach? Should he keep the gold for himself in the event that there is any more? What about Junior?

"Where did you get this?" asked Jimmy.

"From a guy at show in Ft. Myers a coupla' months ago. Said he found it along the Caloosahatchee River one day when he was fishing up near LaBelle. Said he got out of the boat to take a leak and stretch his legs a little and there it was stickin' out of the mud and shinin'. He didn't think much about it at first, thought it was a piece of broken glass or a mussel shell stickin' up but once he looked closer he seen what it was."

"Was there more?" asked Jimmy.

"Nah, after he found it he looked all over real good and didn't see anything else. He went back home and after a few days borrowed a coupla' thousand dollars against his trailer and bought a nice metal detector. He took it back out there and spent two days and never found nothin'. His old lady divorced him over the metal detector so I give him a hundred dollars for it to try and help him out."

"Did you ask him about anything else lying around like pottery shards, bone, bits of charcoal?"

"He said there was nothing else. I don't know if he would have recognized anything else though. Hey…do you need a good metal detector, I know where there is one that's cheap," said Junior.

Jimmy didn't answer Junior about the metal detector. "Where did this come from?" asked Jimmy holding the vertebra with the spear point in it up to the light again.

"I got that from a dude runnin' a dragline for the state. They been workin' some sort of restoration deal, filling in a canal to help save the Everglades. They way down in Hendry County, out east somewhere next to the saw grass where it joins up to the rockin' dubya ranch. He been walkin' that machine south for almost eight months now, figgers if he takes his time, plans for some breakdowns ever now and then he'll have a job with the state for at least four more years."

"That's a nice story but did he tell you where he got it exactly?"

"Well, he had a whole box of stuff in the back of his truck. Mostly it was shit like sharks teeth, whale bones, mastodon teeth, stuff like that."

Jimmy took a soil and conservation district map out of the cabinet and unrolled it. He put ashtrays down on each corner to hold it in place. "Where?"

"He started finding some of the big animal bones here," said Junior putting his index finger on the map. "A couple of months later he was sittin' there eating his lunch up on the bank and he found the neck bone here," he placed his finger on another spot.

Jimmy's mind raced. He prided himself

in knowing every site from Key West to Apalachicola, every rise in the ground more than a foot but this spot was new to him. He closed his eyes and sat back for a while and thought. He started putting together a mental picture of life in 1513, of the sites he knew. He recalled what he knew from studying the archives of the Spanish and what their scribes had to say. It was a trance like experience for him and he let it guide him. It rarely let him down.

"Junior, this is a big deal. If I tell you it is a big deal then you believe me right?"

"You betcha' Jimmy. We have worked a couple of big deals before. What are you thinking?"

"There was a network of villages from the Keys, Miami, up the east coast all the way to Jacksonville, and the same thing on the west coast to about the north side of Tampa," said Jimmy. "It was like a kingdom. Here is where the king lived," he said pointing to a spot near San Carlos pass at Ft. Myers Beach.

"I don't know what you're getting at," said Junior.

"I know but just listen, it will make sense. Back during the Indian war U.S. soldiers camped on a mound on the shore of Fisheating Creek. Hell, we done it as kids, you and your family done it too. It was a nice place and the fishing was good. Lots of people did it."

"Yeah, I member goin' there. I member when it got tore up too, it really pissed of the old timers around here."

"Junior, do you remember why they tore it up?"

"Not really, I was just a kid."

"The State came in ahead of the land owner because the owner was going to do it anyway. State figgered if they could swing some kind of a deal with 'em they could at least take a scientific look at the site and try to interpret it. What happened was they took twenty million dollars worth of Spanish gold out of it that the land owner ended up with. The State got to survey the site, catalog all the material remains, and preserve the stuff that was still intact that was buried in the muck."

"So what's your point? You want to go back in there and see if they missed something? I doubt that. They picked that place over like a bunch of buzzards on a dead cow. 'Sides that, the people who own that place will blow your head off and leave you out there for the gators, I done mixed it up with them once in my life and I ain't doin' it again especially since there is nothing left out there."

"Listen to me, that's not what I am trying to say. This place was thought to be a ceremonial center far from the political centers along the coast. That's what the experts think anyway. Here is what I think it was. It was the meso-American equivalent of a bank vault."

"Yeah and the modern Americans robbed it, end of story," said Junior.

"Hear me out. In fifteen forty a Spanish expeditionary party got jumped around here," said Jimmy placing his finger roughly at the mouth of present day Fisheating Creek.

"The scribe and two others were the only ones who survived the attack or were not kidnapped. The scribe of course wrote down the whole thing as soon as it was safe to do so. He described the attackers as tall fit men covered in tattoos and 'adornments' who were 'fierce'. Ten years later and fifty miles to the south of where that attack happened, another expeditionary party crossed paths with another group similar to the one I mentioned. This time instead of attacking, they turned their canoes south and left."

"Wonder why?" asked Junior.

"No know one knows. Maybe there were more Spaniards than they wanted to deal with. Maybe it was because the area was more open and the Spaniards had guns. Maybe they didn't want to risk it for some other reason," said Jimmy.

"I still don't see your point."

"When they ransacked the Fisheating Creek Mound they found strong evidence that there was another site similar to it further south. No one knows what the evidence was for that idea because the man who came up with it shot his self in the head one night. Found him dead in the parking lot of a bar outside Fort Myers."

"Do you think there is another mound?" asked Junior.

"Of course I do," said Jimmy.

"Here's what I cain't figger out. Why would a bunch of Indians in the fifteen hundreds or sixteen hundreds want a bunch of gold? They didn't use money, didn't have no use for it. Why would they stash so much of it and what did they intend to do with it, make fishing lures?"

"They saw how the Spanish reacted to it. They knew they would do anything, risk anything to get their hands on it. It was political insurance for them. They could lead and manipulate the Spanish all over hell and back with the promise of a few chunks of gold. People ain't that much different today," said Jimmy.

"Where did they get it?" asked Junior.

"From the Spanish, that's the irony of the whole thing. When the Spanish ships wrecked along the Keys and the east coast it was in shallow water. They would either hire the locals or capture them and force them to help salvage the ship. It didn't take long before the locals realized that they could go along with it and once the salvage operation was done, kill their captors, take the gold and other things back to the village and go on with life. The gold became an item of tribute because all of the tribes had to pay a tribute to the king of this group of fierce Indians at San Carlos. All the gold that came pouring in as tribute was packed up and sent to this 'bank' or 'banks' out here," said Jimmy pointing again at the map. "The gold underwater ain't nothin' compared to what is buried along the coast and inland in these mounds. The underwater guys have found their fair share mostly from wrecks in deeper water from ships that broke apart because they were too heavy. The spoils from the shallow water wrecks against the reefs were carted off a long time ago before the Spanish even got the word back to Spain that there had been a loss. That's why so many of the so called salvagers never find anything but a few old rusted cannons and an anchor every now and then."

"I think I am beginning to get the picture

now Jimmy. What is it that you think we ought to do?"

"We aren't going to do anything. You are going to get back down there and pay your dragline buddy a visit and take a look around. See if you can work some kind of a deal to go out there and spend a couple of days, and nights too. Dig some test holes and see what comes up," said Jimmy.

"That sounds like a good plan," Said Junior.

"Let me know when you plan on going out there. I want to know something in a week after you leave for that canal bank," instructed Junior.

"I sure will. It's kind of excitin' thinking that I may be the first 'arkeelogis't to make a big discovery in a long time. Everbody will be amazed that I figgered it out," said Junior beaming.

"Maybe someday Junior but not now. You keep your mouth shut and do what you do best. Go low and slow. Don't let anybody see you or think that you are diggin' because if you are found out it will be the end of the story. If you find what I think you will find it will be plenty enough to take care of us for three lifetimes," said Jimmy. "You can be famous after you're dead."

"Okay, I'll get to work tomorrow. I'll call my buddy and pay him a visit and go out to the work site. I will call you when I know what day I'm going out there, how long I plan to stay, and when I'll be back," said Junior.

With that, Jimmy shook his hand and

gave him a roll of fifteen one hundred dollar bills for the material Junior provided. He knew that in twenty four hours he will turn those fifteen hundred dollars into seventy five hundred dollars. Junior tipped his dirty hat and opened the door of the motor home and stepped outside.

The other man with Junior was called 'Hole'. He sat patiently outside waiting for Junior to make his deal. Hole was Junior's assistant. He was just a big as Junior but not quite as bright. Jimmy figured he got his nickname because he was a digger employed by Junior whenever they excavated a potential site. When Hole stood up he had a paper napkin tucked into his shirt and he had a sparerib in his hand. Jimmy could see his face shining in the pale light of the Japanese lanterns. It was covered in pork fat from the ribs. There were at least eight empty beer cans at the table he was sitting at.

"Hole, why don't you ever try and look presentable? Don't you get tired of lookin' and smellin' the way you do? I know you do some pretty dirty work but damn son, you don't work all the time," said Junior.

Hole just looked at Junior then down at his shirt, then back up a Junior. "We gotta' job?" he asked.

"We got a job and we are headin' south early. If I'm goin' to ride for eight hours with you in the morning, you'd best get cleaned up. This could be a big job Hole. Keep quiet, do what I ask you to do and if it pans out you will be set," said Junior. "If you get caught or if the state shows up because you said something by accident, Jimmy will kill you and it won't be fun I promise."

Just like he predicted, Jimmy made a few phone calls and had all of the pieces sold within a few hours. He would leave Tallahassee in a day or two and start making deliveries. He would start in Tampa then head over to Sarasota to see one of his 'artsy' clients then head down to Naples where he would meet one more and then spend the night. On his second day he would drive across the state to Miami where he would meet up with one of his most loyal customers and one that he had been trading with for nearly thirty years, Dr. Rodriguez or to Jimmy, simply Rudy. He would have lunch with Rudy, maybe a nice Cuban sandwich down in Coconut Grove, maybe some coffee and a smoke. Afterwards he would show Rudy the pieces, collect his money and head back home to Kissimmee. Jimmy always saved the very best for Rudy because he never bickered with him about money. Rudy trusted Junior but he also knew the value of what Junior was selling. Rudy was the consummate collector of antiquities and he knew the value of everything he liked to collect and his passion was pre-Columbian art.

Chapter 3

It was late winter in Florida. Hunting season was over and the Rockin W Ranch was in a period of peaceful bliss. The bunk house at the cow camp was only half full because many of the cowboys tool this chance to vacation or rodeo or simply visit with friends and family. This was the time of year when the Widon family gathered at the camp with their friends and family. Most of the people there had been there for the last week of hunting season and would stay on another week during the cooler weather to help build fence, hang gates, move cattle, and tidy up before the bulls were moved. The cows were fat and happy.

Doc Widon had been in the camp for nearly a month. Doc's sister and her husband joined him along with their son 'Sport' during the last week of the regular hunting season along with Jake Alvarez and his girlfriend Jenny. Jake and Jenny had been together nearly two years and she had a young son named Adam from a previous marriage who joined them as well.

Doc and Jake had met again for their annual camp out but this time it was a little less rough and a lot more civilized. Jake's Uncle Bobby came out as well to visit camp and just be with old friends. He hadn't seen Jake or Doc for a couple of years, ever since fate put them together at Big Cypress when a plane full of bad guys crashed their fishing expedition.

Nights were a special time in the cow camp. Everybody there could cook and mealtime was always special. Most nights there would be something sizzling on the coals of a live oak fire.

Afterwards some of the people in camp would ride out into the wilderness on ATV's and look at the animals that were looking back at them. Deer, bob cats, and every now and then a bear or a wild hog would get caught in the headlight and if the light hit the retina just right their eyes would glint back light mirrors. The youngsters loved this activity but what they loved more than anything was when Bobby would stoke up a big fire and tell stories. By day Bobby would gather a pickup load of lightered pine while helping the cowboys far out on the ranch. The pine was the crystallized heart of pine trees that were killed suddenly by lightening or some other reason while the sap was up. When set on fire, the pieces burned brightly and gave off wisps of dark smoke that kept any wintertime bugs at bay. The smell was indescribable and it evoked memories of campouts, childhood, and fellowship amongst the people in camp.

"Uncle Bobby tell us a story," said Sport whose given name was really David. He got the nickname Sport early in his life and it just stuck. He was after all a Widon and was a natural at being a cowboy as well as an outdoorsman. Doc had spent a great deal of time with Sport on many cattle round ups and hunting and fishing trips.

"Tell us an Indian story again Uncle Bobby," said Sport. "You're an Indian; you must know lots of stories."

"Yeah," said Adam. "Tell us a scary story about Indians like you did last year."

"What scary story?" asked Bobby.
"There are no scary Indian stories; there are just

true Indian stories."

"Okay, I can tell you about the stories of how the Indians here came to be, or I can tell you about the clans, or how the alligator got his tail," said Bobby.

"No, we don't want to hear about any 'once upon a time' story, I mean we like them and everything but we want to hear about what it was like a long time ago," said Sport.

"Yeah, like Huckleberry Finn stuff, you know," said Adam. Bobby sat quietly for a while and thought about it while the two boys stared at him in the firelight. They poked at the coals in the fire with sticks that they had used earlier to roast marshmallows on. Bobby thought hard because the night before the boys had put a chicken snake in his sleeping bag and this might provide a moment of retribution if he played it well. When he found the snake he didn't say anything, he simply picked it up and tossed out the back door of the camp house. All through the next day the boys snickered and asked him how he slept, if his sleeping bag was comfortable, and if it had any holes in it. When one of them asked a question, the other one would look away and tried not to laugh. Bobby played along with them but never mentioned the snake. Now that he thought about it he knew that he could brew up a story that fourteen year old Sport and twelve year old Adam couldn't resist and when he closed the trap on them he would give them a scaring like they never had in their lives and one that they would tell their kids about one day.

"You know that some of the hammocks out here are haunted, at least that's what I was told when I was a kid," said Bobby.

"No way, we don't believe in no ghost stories Uncle Bobby," said Sport.

"Yeah, I looked up ghost on the internet and I didn't see anything that scared me, I don't believe in them either," piped Adam.

"What kind of self respecting ghost would be on the internet?" asked Bobby of the two of them. "How could a ghost be on the internet? You can't film them, you never know where they are going to turn up and suppose you did have a camera and you saw one, they could disappear before you could say jack rabbit."

"How do you know?" asked Sport.

"Because I was told about it and I saw one before," said Bobby fully expanding on a tall tale that he was making up as he went along.

"Where did you see a ghost," asked Sport.

"Well, right here," said Bobby.

"No way," said Adam. "We don't believe you," he added speaking on behalf of both of them.

"What kind of ghost would live here in this cow camp anyway?" asked Sport.

"Well I reckon it was an old cowboy ghost. That's what it looked like to me anyway," said Bobby recognizing that he was losing his argument very fast.

"Yeah right! Ha-ha, cowboy ghost, did he have a ghost horse and a ghost dog with him too? Uncle Bobby, that's not the kind of story we want to hear," said Sport.

"Ya'll come over here and sit down. I think I know what you guys are talking about.

You're too old to believe in spooks but you want to hear a story that might be true and might be scary in some kind of real way."

"Yep," said Adam.

"Yeah, you know stuff that's interesting and kinda' scary in a way. Not like little kid scary but like it could be real and might be spooky to somebody like Uncle Doc," said Sport.

"Uncle Doc said you used to scare him and Jake all the time when were kids by sneaking up on them when they were camping out and stuff," said Sport.

"Yeah...scared the crap out of both of 'em a couple of times. Did they ever tell you about it?"

"Yep, told us about the time you fell out of the boat on purpose and pretended to drown and left both of them wondering what happened to you."

"Yeah, that scared them. They were fussing about something all afternoon, I don't remember what it was and I told them if they didn't stop I was just going to jump overboard. So they kept on and on and I jumped in. Well, I made it look like a fell in. I swam up under the bow and just hung out there for a while until they got nervous. Pretty soon they quit bickerin and started lookin' for me and they got nervous. They were both leanin' over the bow lookin' in the water when I jumped up and pulled them both overboard with me. It was only three feet deep and both of 'em' could swim like fish but it scared 'em' so bad they stopped fussing and never did it again."

"Yeah, they told us about that and also about the time you left them at the airboat camp to go get supplies and then after dark you snuck up on the camp and made noises like some kinda' swamp monster and threw rocks on the roof and stuff," said Adam.

"That was a good one. I made sure I took all the shotgun shells out of the camp before I pulled that one off cause by that time both of them were pretty good shots," said Bobby. He was beginning to craft a plan for scaring the two boys as he was talking to them.

"You know a long time ago, I mean a long, long time ago there was Indians all over this country down here."

"We know that, they taught us about it every year while we were in elementary school," said Sport.

"Yeah I really loved learning about that stuff and just when it got good they quit so they could teach us about stuff that happened in Europe and Russia and other places. Real boring then, I think they should teach about Indians and stuff every year in school," said Adam.

"I agree," said Bobby. "You can't ever learn too much about where you live."

"I guess we're just going to have to rely on you to hear the good stuff Uncle Bobby. So what 'bout those Indians that lived here?" asked Sport.

Bobby slid down off the log he was sitting on and sat down in the sand. He adjusted his back against the log and threw another chunk of wood on the fire. Jake hollered across the yard of the camp house at him, "Don't be telling those youngins any lies now like you did us."

"Hey, watch yourself, it never hurt you guys!" said Bobby.

"So, yeah, there were lots of Indians here a long time ago."

"For how long Uncle Bobby?"

"A long time. Even back during the ice age. Florida was a lot bigger then too and so were the animals."

"No way, how do you know that?" asked Adam.

"Because boy, I learned about it in college."

"You went to college?" asked Sport.

Bobby picked up a pine cone and threw it at him.

"Listen junior, I've done a lot of things you don't know about. That's why I am smarter than you. That's why you gotta' keep working hard so you get smarter than me one day and smarter than your uncle Doc too."

"So ten thousand years ago Florida was maybe fifty miles bigger on the Gulf side. They found fire circles where the Indians lived and camped way out in the Gulf. It was all dry land when all the water was locked up in the last ice age. They hunted giant animals like mastodons. Animals hunted them too like wolves and saber toothed cats."

"What happened to them?" asked Adam.

"Nobody knows. Maybe the weather, maybe competition, maybe they moved or just changed. We know that they were very good at what they did. They made very good tools and weapons."

"Were they here, I mean right here where we are now?" asked Sport.

"I don't know. Probably not but there were lots of Indians all over the place around here from about two thousand years ago all the way until white people got here. There are village sites and burial sites all over down here. Even on this ranch," said Bobby.

"No way!" said Adam.

"Yes way. Right here on this ranch."

"Where, how come we never saw it? How come nobody ever took us there and told us about it if there were Indians living here?" asked Sport.

"You've been there. Both of you have. You just never knew what you were standing on. You gotta' learn to look down around here if for nothing else just to look out for snakes," said Bobby.

"When did we see it? Where is it?"

"I don't know, maybe four years ago when Jake and Doc took you two knuckleheads turkey hunting. They put you in a blind at four thirty in the morning and you talked until the sun came up then fell asleep. When they came to get you there were turkeys all around but you guys were sawing logs by that time," said Bobby with a chuckle.

"I member that! What was it then? An old Indian village?" exclaimed Sport.

"Probably," said Bobby.

"Where is it? It was dark when we went there and I don't think we been back since then," said Sport.

Bobby pointed back over his shoulder in

the fire light, back to the east. "You know that canal back over there about four miles or so? The one that they are filling in? Well, that used to be a river until the nineteen twenties when they put in to dry this country up so the people from up north could build houses and farmers could farm. If you look at one of those NASA pictures from space you can see how the canal cut a straight line right down the old river. You can still make out the meanders but you gotta' look close. There are old village sites all up and down those old meanders. The draglines went right through some villages and some burials too."

"How do you know all that Uncle Bobby?"

"I went to college. I'm an Indian too," said Bobby.

"We want to go out there and see," said Sport with Adam chiming in as well.

"Well, I thought about taking you out there but I think you might get too scared," said Bobby. He knew he had them now; his trap was set to pay back the snake in the sleeping bag stunt.

"I don't know boys. There is nothing out there that'll get you but I heard of some people comin' back changed like they saw something they would never forget but would like to forget," said Bobby.

Both of the boys perked up and scooted in closer to Bobby. They watched his face for a sign that he was going to tell them a truly scary tale.

"What is it Bobby, what kind of stuff happened? Who did it happen to?" asked Adam.

"It happened to me, that am who," said Bobby now at the start of his tall tale. He looked at both the boys with a stern face and a look of seriousness they weren't used to seeing.

"So what happened?" asked Sport again, the anticipation was making him fidget.

"I can't tell you."

"What? What do you mean you can't tell us? We been sittin' here through all this, hoping that you would tell us a story that would spook us and now you can't tell it?" asked Sport, now pleading.

"It's not that, I just gotta' give you a little background first. If I don't then you'll think I am pullin' your legs."

"He's fakin'," said Adam.

"Uncle Bobby are you fakin'?" asked Sport.

"No, I'm not fakin'. I'm just trying to make sure in my head that you two can stand this and won't go crying to your mammas after I finish telling it."

"Yeah, right Uncle Bobby. Ha ha, we don't run to our mammas and cry about little ole ghost stories."

"Alrighty then," Bobby started out. "A long time ago, not like the last ice age long time ago but more like four or five hundred years ago there was a big band of very fierce Indians that lived where Ft. Myers Beach is today."

"Yeah, we heard about them in school. The Calusa," said Adam.

Sport piped in, "They made all sorts of stuff like masks, and weapons, and pottery and they ate real good because of all the fish."

"So you know a little about them. What else did they teach about them?"

"Well, they had really big canoes that could go on the ocean, and now they are all gone," said Sport.

"Did they teach you in school how we came to know what we do about them?" asked Bobby.

"Nah, not really. They told us about this guy who dug up a bunch of their stuff. It was an expedition that happened a long time ago," said Adam.

"There's a lot more to it than that. When the Spanish traveled or went on an expedition they always took someone along to record they journey. They called them scribes. They wrote down everything and they drew pictures too. It was kinda' like a news reporter going somewhere today. When they reached Florida in fifteen thirteen they had scribes with them too," said Bobby to the boys whose eyes were glued to him in the flickering light.

"So they wrote stuff down about the Calusa people? So? asked Sport.

"They did write stuff down; they wrote about a thousand armed warriors, the canoes, and the chief. They wrote a lot of other stuff down too."

"Like what?" Uncle Bobby.

"One of those writers got himself caught by the Calusa. He lived with them for seventeen years. They came after him once but he already got himself a bunch of tattoos and an Indian wife. He didn't want to go back with them. He stayed on and on their second trip, seventeen years after he got caught, he finally went back," said Bobby.

"That's cool, I wish I got caught by a band of Indians and could learn all that great stuff about fishing and hunting and how to make tattoos," said Adam.

"My point is that this fellow that they caught kept writing and he never stopped. When he got back to Spain the stuff he wrote got sealed up in the archives," said Bobby.

"What else did he write about?" asked both boys simultaneously.

Bobby was now in his best tall tale telling form. "Well, he wrote a lot about ceremonies, like when somebody died."

"See, I told you Adam, Bobby is the best story teller around. What about when somebody died?"

Bobby ratcheted up the story, "It was a big deal. When that happened they needed a ceremony. The whole village, people from other villages, and a bunch of the warriors took part. If it was a real important person, people from a long way away came but the most important person there was the medicine man."

"What did he do?" asked Sport.

"He kept everybody safe," whispered Bobby.

"Safe from what? asked both boys.

"Lots of things, mostly spirit stuff with one exception," said Bobby.

"What kind of exception?" asked Adam.

"There's this old folk tale that is supposed to be from Tennessee about this female creature that was built like a woman and walked on two legs but it is more like the cross between a panther and a human. In Tennessee and other parts of the south they call it a wampus cat. They say it came about because this beautiful Indian woman wanted to know what the men talked about when they went hunting so she got the skin of a panther and put it around herself and followed the men. When she got caught the medicine man bound the skin of the panther to her forever. She is supposed to be out there still."

"We saw a carving of a panther that looked like a woman that those expedition people dug up. They called it the Key Marco Cat," proclaimed Adam.

"That may be a carving of a wampus cat. The only place that has panthers is down here. The Spanish scribe called it pantera though he never saw it. He only saw its eyes. He saw lots of carvings of it too but only one was ever found."

"That is cool Uncle Bobby. So you are saying that there is a cat woman out at that old village?"

"No, I don't think so but I haven't finished telling my story yet. When someone died from the village, the medicine man would go out into the woods and find the spirit of the dead person. He would wear one of those masks like the expedition people dug up. When he found the spirit he would drive that spirit into what the Spanish guy said was a 'lesser' animal until it got down to a snake or a turtle or a bug, maybe a bird. Then it was safe."

"Safe from what?" asked Sport.

47

"The wampus cat, the panther woman. If she ever got to the spirit first it would empower her to live another hundred years or more maybe. Anyway, if she couldn't find a spirit, she would just go take one. That's why the Calusa would stake some poor Spaniard or some captive out in the swamp twice a year. It kept her from killin' but it didn't do anything about her taking over the spirits of people who just died."

"So she is here. She could be here couldn't she?"

"No, but the medicine man had the same power and he may still be here. No one has seen a wampus cat around here in at least eighty years. But they have seen signs of a medicine man."

"What are the signs Uncle Bobby, what are the signs?"

"Simple, the wampus cat has yellow eyes when you shine a light in them. The medicine man has blood red eyes and they shine like a gators."

"Red eyes don't mean nuthin'," said Adam. "There are red eyes all over the place."

"It does matter when they are six feet off the ground," said Bobby. Both of the boys looked at each other, then back at Bobby.

"I think we need to plan a camp out for you two out at the old village," said Bobby.

The boys looked at each other and extend their hands in an exaggerated high five motion.

"That would be so cool Uncle Bobby, when can we do it?"

"We? There is no we. You mean when can you and Adam camp out there?"

The boys looked at each other again and Bobby picked up on just a tiny bit of apprehension. They were scared but would never admit it.

"How about tomorrow night?" asked Sport.

"How about tomorrow night and the next night?" responded Bobby. "If you stay out there for two nights, and you don't come back to the camp house for any reason except your hurt, snake bit, or dyin', I'll give you fifty dollars each."

"Deal," said Adam.

Sport looked at him, hesitated then extended his hand to his Uncle Bobby, shook Bobby's hand and proclaimed, "Deal."

Everyone else in the camp had already turned in an hour ago. The boys got up and dusted themselves off and walked as quietly as they could into the house. They whispered back and forth for a long time about the stories Bobby told and about how much fun they would have camping at the village site. They snickered back and forth about what they were going to do with the money that they were going to get from Bobby. Eventually they fell asleep.

Junior Davis had been in Clewiston for nearly a day and a half trying to hook up with his buddy Donny Gillis the dragline operator. He had called Donny while he was still in Tallahassee and told him that he wanted to come down and hunt fossils out where he was working. Donny loved to hunt fossils and had a trove of petrified antlers, bones, sharks teeth, turtles, and all kinds of shells. When Donny heard that Junior was interested in fossil hunting he was thrilled.

"Hell yeah buddy, anytime you want, come on down," he told Junior. "Matter a fact, the dragline is broke down right in the middle of a big pile of fossils, lots of shells and stuff. I found a giant shark tooth out there 'fore I come to town yesterday. I'll wait for you to give me call when you get here and we'll head out there."

"I'll probably be there sometime tomorrow," said Junior never thinking to ask Donny where he would be when he got down there. Donny lived near Kissimmee but pulled a camp trailer out to job sites so he could keep the motel money the state provided him to himself.

Junior and Hole got to town in the early afternoon. They found a campground next to the big lake and set up housekeeping. They had a spacious tent, the site had electricity so they could use the fans to keep cool with at night if they needed them. After they got settled they went into town to get provisions which consisted mostly of beer, some charcoal, several packages of smoked sausage, a loaf of white bread, and some sweet pickles. They came back to camp and cooked and ate. They drank lots of beer.

"Whatcha' lookin' for down here Junior?" asked Hole.

"I'm thinking we might stumble on some grave goods, maybe some points like arrow heads, knives, and spear points. Maybe other stuff too like pottery, hell, you never know," said Junior. "This is private property though and you have to be very careful. If you get caught you need to ditch what's in your pocket and lie your ass off and tell them you was lost or broke down or something. I ain't goin' back to jail for no bag of rocks do you understand me?"

"Yup, I know whatcha' mean, me neither, ain't worth it. I brought the stuff we need for workin' at night, we'll be fine," said Hole.

Junior spent most all of the next morning and part of the early afternoon in a local truck stop- jook joint-bar playing pinball machines and leaving messages for Donny. Every time he had a beer he would call and leave another message. Somewhere around beer nine Donny picked up the phone.

"Where the hell you been?" asked Junior.

"Man I was waitin' on you. Where you stayin'?"

Junior told him and Donny broke out in a laughing hoot over the phone when he realized they spent the night within a quarter of a mile from each other.

"Man, look out of yer tent to the left and you could probably see the top of my camper stickin' out over the bull rushes," said Donny. "Why don't y'all come on over and I'll show you some of the stuff I found out there."

"We'll be right there," said Junior as he hung up the phone.

Junior tossed the keys to the truck to Hole who hadn't had anything to drink all day.

"This is just a little insurance in case I was to get stopped by the cops down here while I was drunk," said Junior. "Be careful and don't get us in a wreck."

"You the boss," said Hole as they turned left out of the dusty parking lot and headed toward town and the campground.

When the two made it to Donny's camp trailer he had several cardboard boxes out on the picnic table that came with the site. The table was made out of concrete and had thick leathery smears of ketchup and other things on it from scores of previous guests.

"Ya'll get out and come on over and take a load off," said Donny. "Take a look at some of the stuff I found out where I been workin'," he said as he hefted a perfect mastodon tooth from the first box.

"That's a nice one," said Junior. "Want to sell it to me?"

"Nah, that's how come I'm in town now. Ever few weeks I call the boss and tell them I had some kind of a break down and I have to leave for a coupla' days to get parts. It ain't ever somthin' serious, just stuff that I can fix is what I tell 'em. Once I have a box full of bones I come into town and I call some of the folks I know that collects this stuff and they come out, I sell it, then I go back to work. I made nearly twice as much money ever week for the last month than I did running that machine. It works out good. When I get back out there I work it hard for a couple of days and nights cause they can tell from space where the machine is and they think they know how far along I should be. So far it has worked out pretty good with the whole breakdown story and ain't none of them offered to come out to check on the machine themselves."

"When you want to head back out there?" asked Junior.

"I gotta' meet some folks tomorrow and try and get rid of some of this stuff. It would be a good day to get some supplies ready. We can head back out there the day after tomorrow. It ain't hard to get there," said Donny as he pulled out a map or the area and pointed to a spot at the end of a twenty mile long dirt road that was arrow straight.

"All right then, me an Hole will go fishin' in the morning and we'll go into town to get some supplies together and meet you back here in the evening."

"That sounds good. We can cook out tomorrow night, drink some beers and head out the next morning," said Donny.

"Sounds like a plan."

Chapter 4

The next day Bobby took both the boys into to town to outfit their trip. They had found a pretty respectable two man dome tent at the local discount mega store. They boys spent a long time picking through items and imagining uses for them. There were waterproof matches, case for the matches, all sorts of fire starters, stuff in a packet that promised to burn even if it was raining.

"Hey Uncle Bobby, do you think we need this?" asked Sport as he handed him a collapsible stove that held a small pot of jellied alcohol.

"Now what in the world would you do with something like that? I guess you could heat up some beanie weenies but it looks like a great way to burn your tent down to me," said Bobby.

"What do you think about this compass?" asked Adam.

"You have a GPS on the four wheeler, it comes off so you can carry it with you. The batteries last four days on one charge. You live in Florida, its flat as a pancake and you know where the sun comes up and you know where the camp house is," said Bobby.

He took the boys around to the aisle that had all of the headlights, flashlights, LED's, signaling devices, and other cool miniaturized items. Bobby picked up two LED headlights with elastic bands, two LED lights that could be clipped on the brim of a cap, and enough batteries to last the boys for several weeks. He picked up an electric lantern and a couple of one pound propane cylinders and some spare mantles for a gas lantern that was back at the camp.

"Light, this is what you need. You can't do anything if you can't see," said Bobby.

They finished their shopping spree by throwing in four dehydrated dinners in Mylar bags, four packages of ramen noodles, some beanie weenies, some cookies, beef jerky, a loaf of bread, and a pack of sausages. The last thing Bobby put in the basket was a plastic tarp and two space blankets.

Once back at the camp house Bobby told the boys to get the rest of their gear together and that he would check what they had gathered before they left. The boys selected a three quart aluminum pot with a lid, a couple of forks, a ling handled spoon, and a plastic basin. They each rolled up their sleeping bags tightly and tied them into a bundle. They each packed a towel, a few spare items of clothing, extra socks, and a small grill. Once Bobby looked over their supplies they carefully placed everything into a large plastic bin. Bobby put a small bottle of liquid detergent in it, a pack of butane lighters, and a long handled butane lighter into the box and they closed the lid.

Sport went out to the barn and started up the big four wheeler and brought it alongside the door to the camp house while Bobby put some things or his own into the back of the ranch jeep along with the items he purchased for the camp out. The boys hefted the plastic bin up onto the rack on the back of the ATV and strapped it down with bungee cords.

It was early afternoon by the time the campers set out for the old Indian village site. Bobby took the lead as he drove out of the yard, over a cattle guard and under the large cypress sign with Rocking W Ranch carved into it along with several family brands burned into it. The boys followed behind him as they left the camp and headed into a large pasture with knee high brown grass in it. The first signs of a special winter clover were just starting to show and by the end of February hundreds of cows would be dining their way through it. The jeep stuck to well worn ruts that tended to throw the four wheeler if a tire was caught in it so the boys stayed off the road and to the side. Once they got to the other end of the pasture the road curved gently to the right. The sky was perfectly clear and the air was dry and cool. Soon they arrived at a gate and Sport hopped off the ATV and opened it so Bobby could move through with the jeep. Adam drove the ATV through the gate after the jeep passed and Sport closed the gate and hopped on the back. They were in an area that had not been improved into pasture although it was neat and looked like a scene out of a landscape painting. Cattle grazed here certain times of the year but there was nothing planted here for them. They foraged on roughage consisting of native grasses and other plants. There were pine trees and palmettos on a broad savanna. On the higher ground there were live oaks. Dotting the landscape all over were small dry ponds that filled during the wet season. Waterfowl and wading birds by the thousands flocked to these ponds during wet periods while eagles flew overhead hoping to catch one in flight. This was a special place to Doc's parents just as it had been to his grandparents and their parents. They area was pristine but not without help. Every three or four years the area was burned to rid the landscape of underbrush and dead wood. The fast moving fires were controlled and in the immediate aftermath looked terrible. Within a few weeks life would explode in indescribable green. Grass came back first then the trees, especially the young slash pines. Wildlife poured in almost as fast as the ashes cooled. The area was verdant again. In between burns, a crew of ranch hands would disperse at least once a year to rid the place of invasive plants like pepper trees and melaleuca trees. Hogs were trapped or hunted relentlessly and the one python that was found last year was killed on the spot and turned into a pair of boots, many hat bands, several belts and at least one guitar strap.

The group passed through two shallow water crossings where white sand bottomed creeks flowed south. Since it was the dry season there was only a foot of water in the deepest of the creeks. Before they crossed the last one the boys ran up ahead of Bobby and stopped the ATV and got off to have a look. There were schools of iridescent minnows darting around in a panic and several small largemouth bass swimming about unaware that if rain didn't come soon they would perish along with all the other fish and crayfish in the creek either as a menu item for the herons or as a desiccated skeleton in the cracked mud.

"We forgot fishing poles," said Adam.

"Yeah but there is some line and hooks in the jeep. We can make our own poles and catch some fish and cook them on the camp fire," said Sport.

With just over a mile to go to their destination the boys didn't have a clue where they were going and had only a vague recollection of where they had been. They plodded along behind Bobby until finally the trail broke right. They proceeded out into a vast area bordered on the right by large marsh that had water in it, at least the middle of it did. On the left was an equally large hardwood hammock. They moved along for maybe another quarter of a mile when the trail turned left, up a rise of about three feet and then into the woods. Bobby slowed the jeep to a crawl then stopped it and turned the motor off. The boys pulled alongside of him and shut down the engine on the ATV. Nobody said anything for a minute or two as they waited for the engine noise and motion to leave their bodies. The woods were quiet for the time being because of the interlopers and soon the sounds of life returned. A large wood pecker resumed his work on a new nest in a dead pine tree nearly overhead and it sounded like a machine gun. Other birds quickly resumed their activities and never paid any more attention to the people on the ground."This is it boys," said Bobby.

"Get out and scout out a good camp site and I'll help you get set up."

The boys found the highest piece of ground in the hammock. There were several cabbage trees and a large live oak whose lower limbs swept down almost touching the ground. It was a good climbing tree with dozens of routes up to the top which surely commanded an excellent view of the surrounding woods. There were several wild sour orange trees with fruit in them close by as well. They were in sight of the jeep and Bobby when they motioned him to come over. He pulled the jeep in and the three of them began unloading gear. In no time the tent was up, the lantern was ready for nightfall which was still a few hours away. Once the gear was stashed the boys set about gathering firewood. Once they had most of the dead wood picked up around the camp they joined Bobby in the jeep. He knew where there was an old pile of fence posts that would last them for at least two nights and they all three pitched in to get them loaded into the back of the jeep. Finally Bobby took a detour out to a windmill and filled two five gallon plastic jugs for the boys before they returned to camp.

By the time the sun finally started to set the boys had a fire going. They set the grill across two logs so they could cook the sausage that Bobby bought in town earlier that day. Just before they started cooking they saw headlights bobbing up and down as they grew brighter. Within twenty minutes Doc, Jake, and Jenny joined the intrepid campers for the cook out.

"What do we have here, Daniel Boone and Davy Crockett?" asked Doc as he got out of the truck.

"Haha, funny Uncle Doc."

Doc lifted a cooler full of cold drinks and some extra items for the grill out of the back of the truck.

"How did you two let this old fart talk

59

you into spending the night out here? You know this place is haunted right? Or didn't he tell you?" Doc winked at Bobby who had let him in on the prank earlier that day.

"Doc there is no such thing as ghosts or wampus cats. He's just trying to get us back for puttin' the chicken snake in his sleeping bag night before last. He doesn't think we know. He also hasn't let on anything about the snake in the bag," said Sport.

"Oh, so I get it. He told you a spooky story and then got you to take a bet to stay out here," said Doc.

"Yeah, I reckon he's gonna' come back out here tonight and try and scare us back to the camp house," said Sport.

"You could be right. You know he's pretty tight with a dollar and he's likely to do anything to get you to give up so he doesn't have to pay you," laughed Doc.

"Yeah, we'll play along, we're not scared just in case you're wonderin' Uncle Doc."

"Yeah you are. Don't tell me any different either. He did it to me and Jake. We were all brave and tuff. Yep, did it to us except it was only ten bucks back then. He snuck back on us just as we were going to sleep and scared the hell out of both of us," said Doc laughing.

"Yeah, he don't remember but Adam and me heard that story too. We'll be ready for him."

Jake, Jenny, and Doc left after supper and after the sound of the truck disappeared into the night and the headlights couldn't be seen anymore Bobby walked back over to the jeep. He pulled out a canvas bag and walked back over near the fire and opened it up. He pulled out a jungle hammock like he used when he was in the army in Viet Nam. It was a hammock but it was also a tent with mosquito netting all around it for side and it had a canvas roof on it to protect the user from rain and heavy dew. He hung the hammock between an orange tree and one of the long strong live oak limbs near the fire.

"Whacha' doing Bobby?" asked Adam.

"Well, it's been a long time since I been out here, I thought I would join you and just enjoy the woods for a night."

"What about the bet Bobby? Are you trying to get out of that 'cause you know there is no way we're let you out of that," said Sport.

"No, it's not about that you knuckleheads. It's about being out here. Just consider it a free night. The bet was for two nights, consider this one a gift. Stay out here tomorrow if you want, the bet still stands. Don't tell your moms that I bet with you either."

That night the three of them put their gear to the test on an expedition around the village site. It looked like any other cabbage hammock in South Florida with the exception that it was a couple of feet higher than the surrounding ground and it was rectangular. The whole thing was about the size of a football field. For most people it was imperceptible and it blended right into the rest of the woods and landscape surrounding it.

Around midnight the three of them set out to test their headlights and hike around the perimeter of the site. They had a single shot .22 with them and a couple of bottles of water.

Bobby threw another log on the fire as they left. Not long after leaving camp they startled a foraging armadillo that rocketed off through the dead palm fronds on the ground which made it sound like a much larger beast. The boys cringed a little and Bobby was admittedly a little startled by the headlong rush of the animal. They picked the little armored beast up with their headlights about thirty feet from where they first spooked him. He bucked as he ran and made little grunting noises. He was so intent on running away from whatever it was that scared him that he slammed into the trunk of an oak tree and just stopped. Bobby and the boys were able to approach him then and when they shined their lights in his eyes he just looked back with dazed weepy little eyes until he got his wits back and then he charged off again.

"Scared you didn't he?" said Bobby.

"No, it didn't scare me," said Adam. "How about you Sport, did it scare you?"

"Oh yeah Adam. I thought it was a wampus cat or the ghost of the medicine man looking for her. I'm shaking. I don't think I can sleep tonight," laughed Sport.

Bobby just looked on and realized that he may have met his match in these two. He would either have to work real hard to scare them tomorrow night or he would just have to stay on the porch and accept the fact that he just didn't have it in him anymore.

The back side of the site was fairly open and they could see quite a ways in the moon light.

"See all that over there? The really clear

part? That used to big a big marsh a long time ago. The creek that ran through here brought the water. When they dug the canal it dried up the marsh. That's what they're trying to fix now," said Bobby. He pointed out over the area and swept his hand in a short arc.

"Yeah, we see that. It will be perfect when it gets fixed," said Adam.

"When will it be marsh again?" asked Sport.

"I don't know, they've been working on it for a year and a half and they finally made it down to this point. See that light over there to the left?" asked Bobby pointing again with his finger to a white pinpoint of light about a half a mile away.

"Yep, I see it," said Adam with Sport chiming in too.

"That's the beacon light on the boom of a dragline that is out here working to fill in the canal. They put that little white light up there so crop dusters or other airplanes don't accidentally fly into it at night. Ya'll don't need to be messing around that equipment because it is dangerous. I haven't seen the thing move in a couple of days so it's probably broken down. Just stay away from it, you got no business over there," said Bobby.

"Okay Uncle Bobby. We won't go around it. We understand," said Sport.

Back in camp they stoked the fire one more time and sat around and talked a little more. When it burned down they all three turned in.

"Hey Adam? You awake?"

"Yeah, I am now. What's the matter?"asked Adam.

"Why do you think Bobby stayed out here with us tonight?"

"I wondered about that. Maybe he really is telling the truth and he was worried about us. Maybe there is a wampus cat out here," said Adam.

"Maybe he is worried for us."

"Or maybe he's trying to figure out how to save himself a hundred dollars. Or maybe he just wanted to get away from all those people in camp and relax in the wilderness. Or maybe he had to come out here to figure out how he was going to scare us," said Adam.

"I don't know. I'm going to sleep," said Sport and he rolled over and closed his eyes.

The next morning the campers were up early. Bobby had the fire going and had agreed to make breakfast. He poured out some water into an empty two pound coffee can and put it over the fire. Once it boiled he threw in a couple of scoops of coffee.

"Why don't you guys take a ride around the place in the daylight? You went around the whole place at night, now go see what it looks like in the light," said Bobby.

With that, the two boys hopped on the four wheeler and took off to explore the hammock. They rode around the entire site then crisscrossed it several times. They rode out along the old creek channel behind the levee of the canal. They could see the dragline in the distance. They stopped along the old creek bank to pick at the dirt with sticks. They dug out a couple of white fossilized conch shells and another that looked like some sort of whelk. They found some bones of turtles that had long ago turned to stone. They put these items in a box on the four wheeler and returned to camp hungry.

"That didn't take long," said Bobby. "You must have smelled food."

"Look what we got Uncle Bobby," said Sport as he took the fossils out of the box on the four wheeler.

"That's pretty cool. You guys should pay real close attention and you might find an arrow head down there. When we get back, remind me to show you some of the points I picked up down there when I was a kid."

They finished up breakfast and tidied up the camp. Bobby took his jungle hammock down.

"Alright then. I'm heading back to the camp house. I'll see you guys in the morning if not before," he said with a chuckle.

"Okay Uncle Bobby. We'll see. Thanks for coming out here and showing us around," said Sport.

"Yeah, thanks for taking us to town and for the tent and everything," said Adam.

"That tent stays at the camp house after you guys come in tomorrow. That way it will always be here for you to use or for others to use. Maybe your kids will come out here some day," said Bobby. "The .22 is on top of your sleeping bag with a box of bullets."

Bobby closed the door of the jeep and started the engine. A little puff of blue smoke came out of the exhaust pipe of the jeep that hadn't seen a paved road in over thirty years. He pulled a hundred dollar bill out of his pocket and waved it at the boys as he pulled out of the camp and headed off the camp house.

The boys made two trips back to the camp house during the day. The first one was to get an ax and a hatchet. The second trip was to top off the tank on the four wheeler and pick up a full five gallon can of gas. Each time they came back Bobby would tease them that the bet was over.

Chapter 5

Junior, Hole, and Donny finally made it
out to the dragline after an agonizing two and a
half hour crawl over twenty miles of what had to
be the worst dirt road in the country. Potholes
that could swallow a VW were everywhere.
They hit several of them that caused the front
bumper on Donny's truck to hit the ground. At
least Junior and Hole had some warning by
watching the movement of Donny's truck. Once
they arrived at the work site Junior and Hole
went to work on their camp. They picked a place
on the other side of the canal behind the
remaining levee. It was easy to get to because
Donny had filled in the canal and smoothed the
area flat where it had been. They set up a tent
that they covered with a camouflaged net that
they picked up at an army surplus store. They
were invisible from the air.

While they worked on their camp, Donny
leveled his old camp trailer up and fueled up his
generator with diesel fuel courtesy of the state
tax payers. Junior and Hole ate a big lunch
washed down with semi cool beer then retired to
a pair of folding lawn chairs for a nap. They
were startled awake by the noise of the big diesel
engine of the dragline. Junior was just about to
close his eyes again when he saw the huge
bucket of the machine swing perilously close
overhead dripping mud, water and at least one
fairly respectable snake right on top of their
camp. Junior jumped up from his chair and ran
out in the open yelling and waving his arms.
Donny couldn't hear him over the din of the
machine and he only saw him when he swung

the bucket around and back over the tent camp. Donny idled the machine and climbed down.

"What the hell is the matter with you man?" yelled Junior.

"What do you mean?"

"I mean you just dumped about a hundred gallons of black stinkin' mud and snakes on top of us over there," said Junior.

"I'm sorry man, I couldn't see where you put your tent. I'm used to bein' out here alone. Sorry, I'll work around you," said Donny apologetically.

Junior turned around and walked back behind the low levee to the tent. He went inside to where Hole had set up the little folding card table. Junior pulled the cap off a plastic tube and pulled out several maps. He unrolled them across the table and put rocks on the corners to hold them in place. He put his compass on the table to help get his bearings. The last item he took out was a large satellite image that he special ordered from NASA in which he asked for different elements to be highlighted such as old water courses, limestone formations, and elevations.

They looked at the photo first and quickly determined their location and the general lay of the land. They quickly recognized their position and they knew that the image was fresh because the dragline showed up in it very clearly and it was about 10 miles further north of its current position making the image about six months old. Junior had the image scaled to match the other maps that he had. The maps were printed on the equivalent of tracing paper so he could overlay them on the satellite image, layer by layer until every rock, bush, mud puddle, and tree could be easily picked out. Junior took a compass and drew a circle with their location in the center of it. The diameter of the circle was one mile. From there he took a ruler and drew perfectly straight lines to various landmarks that would be easily identifiable especially in the dark. He numbered each of these lines and when he was finished the map looked like a wheel of a bicycle with spokes radiating out. When he was finished he had about twelve lines drawn which he carefully numbered. Once he was all finished he sat down with Hole to make a plan for the evening hunt. He traced along one of the lines that roughly followed an ancient creek bank to where it ended at the bottom of a small circular rise in the ground of about a foot and a half. The circle was about the same size as one of those round pools that most families with kids own at some point in their lives. Maybe fourteen feet in diameter and perfectly round.

"Later on this afternoon once it gets cooler we're go look for some fossils after Donny knocks off work for the day. I know you hate pickin' up rocks and seashells but just try and humor him. He was nice enough to let us come out here and camp with him. I am going to do the same but I am going to ask him some questions about some of the things he has seen out here and where he saw them," said Junior. "Then we're grill some food and fill him up with whiskey. When he passes out or goes to sleep, that's when you go to work. I'll try and have a look around without having to ask him too many questions."

"You the boss. Since I'm be the one up all night I'm try and get a little shut eye," said Hole.

"Alright sleeping beauty, have a nice nap, I'll come back and get you later."

Junior gathered an olive drab canvas shoulder bag, a trowel, a small folding shovel like the ones that are issued to soldiers, a water bottle, and his army surplus boonie hat and walked out into the sunshine. Donny was working the machine like it was an extension of his arms and hands. Junior just stood there and watched him for a few minutes as the big bucket scooped into the levee, swung widely and deposited its contents into the small canal. He would do this about a dozen times then he would come back and gently smooth the area by dragging the bucket along the ground. This provided a smooth surface much like a bull dozer might leave. Once finished he would engage the large tracks and crawl forward another hundred feet or so and start all over. He could go a fifth of a mile on a good day and nearly a third of a mile on those rare occasions he worked into the night. At the end of his day he would either walk or drive back to his camper depending on how far he was from it. About once a week he would move his camper all the way up to the work site.

Eventually Donny saw Junior standing there and he idled the machine again and climbed down to talk to him.

"Hey Junior! get an early start on fossil hunting this afternoon?"

"Yeah, thought I would come out and have a look around," said Junior cautiously.

"Well, feel free. You can see just from standing here that there is a ton of stuff. Donny pointed all around the area and volunteered to Junior where he found intact fossilized turtle shells, the last mastodon tooth, where most of the petrified antlers were, and best of all where the big shark's teeth came from.

Without asking for it Donny pointed back to the north and towards where the western canal bank once stood and proclaimed, "There's where I found that neck bone with the point broke off in it."

Junior just grinned. It was going to be a good day, and a better night he thought to himself.

"Well thank you Donny, I'm just going to help myself to this stuff. Later on Hole and I plan on cooking some supper on the fire and you're going to be the guest of honor. We wanted to do something to thank you for letting us come out here with you."

"Shoot man, ya'll don't have to do a thing, I just appreciate the company. It gets pretty lonesome out here, especially at night. I quit getting cell phone reception about a week ago, just got too far away from a tower I reckon," said Donny.

"Getting kind of tired talkin' to the armadillos huh?"

"You bet," said Donny.

The two men smiled and then Donny climbed back on the machine and worked two more hours. Junior walked along occasionally stopping to pick something up off the ground. He walked north for a while along the route he planned on sending Hole later. When he was about two hundred yards from where Hole would be working tonight he began to notice small pieces of charcoal about the size if a finger nail. As he got close he stared seeing tiny chips and chunks of pottery undoubtedly smashed to pieces when the canal builders moved through here almost seventy years ago. These were promising clues that something more was nearby that had never been disturbed. He would leave that up to Hole.

Junior walked back to where Donny was working and then on to the south. The ground changed as he walked further south and instead of marl and rock mixed with shells the ground to his right turned to the black muck that made winter vegetables from this part of the world famous. He stopped and looked all the way around in a three hundred sixty degree circle. The map was fresh on his mind and if there was one thing Junior Davis was famous for it was his uncanny ability to commit a map to his memory. Once he came full circle he closed his eyes then slowly opened them again. That's when he saw it. This was another circular area in the landscape, heavily overgrown with all sorts of trees. It was similar to the one that he planned to send Hole to but much larger and much, much higher. The east side had been disturbed by the dragline but not too badly. This is where Donny pointed when he was showing Junior where he found the neck bone. Junior had no doubts that he was looking at an ancient burial site that had previously been undiscovered or simply ignored. Junior looked back over his shoulder to make sure that Donny couldn't see him and he approached the mound. He picked up a piece of a small sapling that had been broken off and stripped of its bark by the heavy equipment operation that has passed through a couple of weeks before. He used that to beat back the vines and the undergrowth as he hacked his way to the top. He also used it to clear the thick yellow webs of the banana spiders and to toss the occasional snake out of the way. Once on top he couldn't see much. It looked much like all the rest of the landscape, only higher. There were live oak trees growing all over it and the one at the very top was an easy climber. Junior took the bag off his shoulders and took a drink of water. He leaned his stick up against the tree and proceeded to climb it. The limbs were perfect and it didn't amount to much more than climbing a ladder. Once at the top Junior was able to get a better idea of what sort of place he was in. To the west there was a vast area of beautiful old growth Florida savanna as far as he could see. He could barely make out green pastures to the north of the woods and he thought he could see a vehicle trail. Immediately to his south he could make out the vague rectangular outline of what had to be a village site. He had seen them before in areas north of here in the Kissimmee Valley. To his east he could see the remnants of a vast marsh. It was an indeterminably huge area. The only reason it was a marsh at one time was because the whole place was just a few inches lower in elevation than the surrounding countryside. Junior closed his eyes and envisioned a substantial population living in a village and going about their daily business of staying alive. He imagined them coming and going by boat, fishing, and growing crops. He began to wonder what happened to them even though he knew. He knew that any thoughts of ancient people always returned to that singular defining moment of when they ceased to exist. It didn't matter who was talking or thinking about them. It could be a scientist, a surveyor, a teacher, and archaeologist, or an inquisitive kid. Maybe it was some sort of intrinsic guilt because their demise began the day the first Spaniard stepped off the ship. Innocence and purity were lost that day and their lives were changed from a culture of self reliance and knowledge accumulated over eons to a life on the defensive. Junior knew full well what happened to them and it was not romantic by any stretch of the imagination.

"Enough crazy thinking," Junior whispered to himself. "If I had been here a thousand years ago, right where I'm at now they'd a slapped an arrow right through me lickity split and someone else would be tryin' to dig me up."

Junior climbed down out of the tree and walked a descending and circling path around the mound until he came to where the dragline had disturbed the east side of it. All around his feet were large chunks of broken pottery. It was finely made and carefully incised with an exquisite pattern. The edges of the relief were sharp and beautiful. The broken edges revealed that the pottery was constructed in three layers. The inner layer was very dark, then the middle layer which was almost orange colored then the outer layer of the dark material repeated.

"They had the time so they must have had plenty to eat," Junior said to himself. He knew that in order to create beautiful things there had to be people dedicated to the craft. In order to be dedicated there had to be a secure food supply and freedom from enemies. "They had a good life here," he whispered to himself.

Junior looked down again and saw several human teeth and a jaw bone scattered about amongst the pottery shards. Without having to look hard, Junior spotted at least two dozen pieces of human bone lying around. It made him wonder how Donny missed those things but not the neck bone he picked up. It didn't really matter to Junior at this point anyway. He was sure he found the mother lode and as far as he was concerned he was the only person on the planet who knew what he was looking at. He walked around and picked up various pieces of bone fragments and put them in a velvet whiskey bag that he had clipped to his belt. When he finished he had four pieces of skull, several teeth and part of a jaw bone in his little sack. He felt bad about it for a little while but then soon forgot about feeling bad once his thoughts turned to the vast sums of money he potentially stood to make. Grave robbing never bothered him for more than a few minutes. When he really thought about what he was doing he felt like he was paying respects in some bizarre way that only he could do.

Junior walked around the mound and let his intuition work for him. He carefully thought out where the likely intact graves would be and he made a mental note of it. Time, that was going to be the factor on this little dig. He would have to work as fast as he could or find a way to stay at the site longer. For the time being he was happy with his discovery and he could worry about the details later.

Junior was about halfway back to where Donny was working when he heard the dragline go silent. Donny closed the door of the operator's cabin and climbed down and stepped off onto the tracks then hopped on the ground. When Junior was sure that Donny saw him he started searching the ground pretending to look for fossils. He stopped and picked up a scallop shell and a small piece of coral.

"Hey buddy! I hope you're finding lots of fossils. What do you think about this place anyway, sure is pretty out here," said Donny.

"Donny this is an amazing place. There are so many shells and stuff just lying around. Man, I would love to spend a couple of weeks out here. I swear, I could just sit on one spot all day long and never get bored."

"I know, it's amazing. You just go along working for weeks at a time sometime and then all of a sudden you hit a place like this and find all these cool shells and bones. My favorite is when I find those mastodon teeth. They bring the most money. Heck, for a really good molar I can get three hundred dollars from the right customer."

"That's a lot of money Donny. Do you

find a lot of them?"

"In the last nine months I have found twelve of them. I sold the best ones right off the bat. I still have five left but I think I can sell those soon. I found a guy in New York City who specializes in stuff like that. Found him on the internet. He wants me to take pictures of them and send them to him and he will send me an offer for all of them at one time. He said he had some stuff he could trade me for too but he didn't say what it was."

"That sounds real good. Tell you what, whatever me and Hole find out here I will split it with you for letting us come out and collect. You can tell me what its worth and you just take whatever you want," said Junior.

"Really? That sounds swell. I really don't get much time to collect because I have to turn in a certain amount of work. I usually tell them that machine is broke down about four days out of the month. I am also off on Sundays but I usually have to go to town and get supplies. I can also shut the machine down in the event we get lightening but this time of year, hell it's been clear for two months and will probably stay this way two more," said Donny.

"That's what I'm sayin' Donny. Hole and I could help. We love it out here and we love to hunt fossils. It would be like a vacation for us," said Junior.

"Yeah, I see what you mean. I sure do enjoy the company. Why don't you guys plan on spending a couple of weeks out here?"

We may just do that. Thanks for the offer. Course I will have to make sure I ain't speakin' for Hole," said Junior.

Hole was just emerging from his nap. He walked out into the afternoon sun and up to where Junior and Donny were talking.

"Have a nice snooze?" asked Junior.

"Yeah I sure did. Getting kinda' hungry now though."

"Me too. What do say we get a fire going and throw some food on the grill?" asked Junior.

"Man I am starved from working all day. That sounds like a real good idea," replied Donny.

Hole walked back over to the tent and came out with a cooler. Junior followed close behind with a couple of folding chairs and the little table he had set up previously in the tent. They walked over to Donny's camp and put the items down. They made two more trips back and forth and once they had all their supplies ready, Hole quickly constructed a fire circle out of some of the larger rocks that were lying about everywhere. Before Hole got back with his first arm load of firewood, Junior had already mixed Donny a double whiskey and cola. Junior went a little lighter on his drink.

In no time, the fire was blazing. Junior put a large grill across the rocks and let it heat up. After brushing it off he took four steaks out of the cooler and seasoned them. He opened a can of pork and beans and put them in a pot off to the side of the grill. He put the steaks on the grill but not before mixing another drink for his good friend Donny. The three of them ate a hearty meal and hardly talked while they ate. Junior took the grill off the rocks and threw a couple of big pieces of wood on the coals and they retired by the flames to drink and talk.

"That was a fine steak if I do say so myself," said Donny.

"Yes indeed," agreed Hole.

"I'm glad we ate when we did because I think I needed some food to help soak up that liquor," said Donny who had just fallen off the wagon for the eighth time in twelve months.

"Yeah buddy, good steak goes well with good liquor. Here, have a beer." Junior handed Donny an ice cold brew from the cooler.

"Tell us more about your fossil business Donny," said Junior.

"Well, there ain't that much to tell that you don't already know. I been picking this stuff up since I was a kid. I used to sell stuff to the tourists during the winter time. I made more money than any of my friends with a paper route and I didn't have to answer to no one. I been my own boss since I was ten. Later on I found out I was getting ripped off by some of the people that was buyin' from me so I decided to learn what different stuff was really worth. I guess I got smart. I started charging more and making up stories about how difficult it was to find the things I was sellin'. Daddy run a dragline when they straightened out the Kissimmee River and he brought home pickup truck loads of old bones and stuff. Guess that's where my interest got started. He died when I was twenty. We had a big barn stacked to the ceiling with fossils so one day I took a couple of boxes and labeled the stuff accordin' to what I thought they were and put prices on 'em. I took them to a fossil show in Ft.

Myers and sold ever bit of it. I made enough money that weekend to buy myself an old truck. The rest is history," said Donny.

"Ever find any Indian stuff, like artifacts?" asked Junior.

"Nah, not really. Ever now and then I may find a point of a broke off arrow head. Your eyes gotta' be trained for that sort of thing and you have to be interested in it. Nope, my thing is fossils. I never sold a single thing that come from an Indian," said Donny.

They continued to talk for two more hours and finally after Junior poured the ninth beer into Donny, he started to get a little blurry and sleepy.

Donny leaned back in his chair and yawned and scratched his head and said, "Man I gotta' get to bed. I got another long day ahead of me and I am starting to feel a little drunk. I don't want to get sick tomorrow smellin' that diesel smoke and listening to that big engine all day. I'll see you fellers in the morning some time and maybe we can hunt fossils tomorrow afternoon."

Donny staggered off to his camp trailer and missed the pad lock three times before he got the key into it. Junior and Hole saw a small light go on and then they heard a loud thud like a hundred pound of hamburger hitting the floor. Donny was out, down for the count. Hole opened the door and stepped inside and covered him up with a blanket and threw a pillow down beside him. He turned off the light and went back outside.

The two hurried back to the tent. Once inside Junior said, "Man do you know what we got out here? This place is pristine. Somehow the canal builders missed it back in the twenties. They came right down the side of a huge village site and mound complex, never even touched it really. We gotta' lot to do, there's pay dirt here."

"I'm with you man. I know the routine. If I get caught, ditch the goods and swear I'm lost. We are out here visiting a friend, doing a little fishing 'fore the canal gets covered up," said Hole.

"You got. Here is the route I want you to explore tonight," said Junior tracing a finger along one of the lines he drew earlier.

"Got it," said Hole.

They both fitted their LED headlights on their heads and checked the bulbs. They had different colored bulbs in them for different conditions. They could burn anywhere from two of the tiny bulbs to all six of them by pushing a button. Hole gathered his shoulder bag and a small shovel and an auger like those used to drill post holes into hard ground. They walked out of the tent and looked back over at Donny's camper and all was quiet.

"Where you goin' tonight?" asked Hole?

"I found an interesting feature just a few hundred yards north of here. I'm gonna' go up there and poke around a little bit and see what I find."

The two men set off in opposite directions.

"Remember, Hole… when that morning sky just starts to lighten, you need to be back here."

"Yes sir, see you in the morning."

81

The two men separated, Junior headed north, Hole went south following the imaginary straight line Junior had traced out earlier.

Chapter 6

Adam and Sport had made one more trip in to the camp house. It was the third trip of the day for the boys. It was late afternoon when they finally hugged their parents and told them they would see them tomorrow. The boys headed back out to their camp. When they got back they stared a small fire and looked over their choice of menu items. After much deliberation they decided on a freeze dried version of beef stroganoff. They didn't really have to cook anything and that was important since they were both hungry now and the sun was starting to set. All they had to do was follow some simple instructions. Boil water, pour it in the bag, roll the top down, wait five minutes then chow down. They got one of the cook pots and estimated the amount of water it would take to prepare the meal. They sat the pot across three rocks they had put in the fire and brought the water to a boil. In a few minutes they were eating. Just at it got too dark to see, Adam lit the lantern they had with then and set the burn low. It cast a soft light across the camp that was not quite as bright as the light from the fire.

"So what do you want to do now?" asked Adam.

"I'm not sleepy. I think we should go huntin'. I think we should go back and find that armadillo that we jumped yesterday with Bobby. We can go back to the same spot and wait for him. We he comes back we'll catch him. We can tie him up to a tree and take him back tomorrow. He can be our pet."

"Yeah, we can do that. We should take

the rifle too just in case," said Adam.

"In case of what?"

"I don't know, just in case. In case any of that stuff Bobby said was really true."

"Okay, we can do that. I don't know how much it will help. It only holds one bullet at a time. And the only bullets we are allowed to have are twenty two shorts so the game wardens don't think we are out here poaching deer or other stuff," said Sport.

The boys waited around for another hour in the dark quiet of the woods. Finally they decided to go in pursuit of their quarry. They retraced their path from the previous evening. They had their headlights on the lowest setting. The dim lights cast weird shadows as they set out into the woods. Both of them were scared just a little but the adrenaline was oh so sweet. They crept along as quietly as possible gently pushing the palm fronds out of their way so their lights could cast a thin beam on what was ahead. They would push forward for a few steps then stop and listen, then move forward again. After about forty minutes or so they stopped and heard the telltale rustling of their fabled quarry. The little armored animal did not rate high on the animal IQ scale but he made up for it in persistence and survivability. The boys listened intently as the leaves rustled then went silent. Then the sounds would start back, a steady rustling and low crunching noise as the animal plowed through the dead palm fronds and leaves. Start, stop, and then start again. One thing was sure to the boys, it was getting closer.

"Hear that?" asked Adam. "It's getting

closer. He's walkin' right back to where we found him last night. Don't shine your light right in his eyes, that'll make him run for sure."

"Okay," said Sport. "Shhh...he's getting closer."The little 'armored one' kept to his business of finding a meal. Nothing distracted him. He came to within five feet of the boys and stopped cold. His terrible vision prevented him from seeing anything of value but his uncanny ability to smell things out of the ordinary set his instincts on high. He sat up on his haunches and sampled the air through his plated little nose. The animal did his best to turn his head within the confines of the shell on his back. Once satisfied that he has a sufficient whiff of whatever it was that he was faced with, he lowered himself back down on all fours, turned around one hundred an eighty degrees and proceeded to haul ass in a remarkably straight line.

"Cowabunga dude!" yelled Sport. He lit off after the animal and actually closed the distance a little bit. "Adam, cut out through the woods, make a big circle and we'll close in on him from different directions."

Adam peeled off to the left and headed out in to the dark woods. He kept himself oriented by the racket Sport was making. Eventually Adam found himself running down the east edge of the village site as hard as he could go. Adam stopped to get his bearings and to listen. He turned off his light in hopes that he would be able to see the dim light affixed on Sport's cap. In the distance he heard a shuffle. The creature had evidently evaded Sport all together or there was another one out there. Shuffle, scuffle, shuffle, and then whump. Adam listened to the noise for about twenty minutes. It was unrelenting and it didn't seem to move. Having lost contact with Sport, Adam decided that it would be up to him to capture this beast single handed and deliver it back to camp. He waited and planned. He decided to wait until he heard the shuffle scuffle noise again then attack. Adam waited for a few minutes then he heard it. Sport was nowhere to be found. The sound came…shuffle….scuffle…whump. It was about thirty to forty five seconds between noises. Then it came again. Adam adjusted his light which was still set on the dimmest setting. Adam took off through the underbrush in an all out run. He made about forty steps and then found himself in mid air. He had run off the side of the mound. He was fully airborne when he crashed feet first into the back of Hole who had been shoveling dirt for the last hour and a half. Hole screamed, Adam screamed and the two of them crashed down on the ground together.

"What the hell!" yelled Hole.

"Yeah, you're right, what the hell," exclaimed Adam before he realized what he said.

"What are you doing out here kid? Who do you belong to?"

"That ain't none of your business mister," said Adam. "Who are you and why are you out here?"

"I don't think I like your attitude boy," said Hole as he grabbed Adam behind the neck.

"You best let go of me you freak. All I gotta' do is yell and it is all over for you. My friends and family will be all over you like you have never seen." said Adam.

"We'll see about that." Hole spun the boy around and took a short piece of rope from his belt and tied Adam's wrists together. "Look, I don't know who you are but I don't need any shit from you tonight. No cops, no game wardens, nobody coming out here."

"What are you doing here? Why do you have that screw thing? Ain't it a little late to be diggin' post holes?"

"You're a little smart ass ain't cha? You know buddy, this is unfortunate 'cause I ain't never had this happen before. I don't really know what to do with you now that we met," said Hole.

"Turn me loose you stinkin' monkey, that's what you could do."

"You know kid, I got lost out here yesterday. Me and a buddy wuz out here fishin'. He went that way and I went this way," said Hole.

"You're full of shit," said Adam, again not believing what just came out of his mouth. He hoped his mom would forgive him once he got out of this mess. "Where's your fishing pole then?"

"That does it. I can't let you go now. I am going to have to take you with me and figger out somthin' else later on. Do you understand me?"

"I think so, but you are a trespasser and you are probably doin' something illegal. When they catch you you're going to be in a world of shit. My family is probably on their way here now."

Sport had been eluded by the armadillo again. He walked a zig zag pattern through the woods. When he heard voice he turned his light off and stopped to listen. He couldn't make out the sounds. It sounded like people talking but he wasn't sure. His senses were heightened and adrenaline was pumping. He lost Adam and was alone for the time being. His heart was racing and his pulse pounded in his temples. He watched to the direction that he sounds were coming from. He thought he heard Adam but he couldn't be sure. He reached into his pocket for a twenty two short. He fumbled the bolt of the little rifle in the dark and finally got the bullet seated in the chamber. He raised his head above the rotten palm stump he had been hiding behind. Adam screamed loudly for Sport.

"Go for help, he's got me!" yelled Adam. In the split second that it took Adam to yell out Hole raised his head. Hole's headlight was fixed with red lenses so he would be less noticeable and only two of the four bulbs were lit. Sport saw the two red bulbs in the darkness and in a fraction of a second had the little gun trained between them. He took a breath and held it and squeezed the trigger. Hole let out a howl as the soft lead twenty two short hit him dead between the eyes up on his forehead. He was stunned at first and staggered around backwards a few steps before catching himself. Both of the lights still burned. He reached up to try and feel his head. The two middle bulbs had been smashed by the round and his head was bleeding. There were a few fragments of plastic and glass imbedded in his forehead but that was about it. That and a lot of blood. At least it seemed like a lot of blood in the dark.

"Go get Jaaa…". That was all Sport heard, then nothing. Hole had wrapped his sweaty arm around Adam's face covering his mouth. Sport listened for a little while then took off for camp on the four wheeler. He hopped on it and headed for the cow camp. He could see the fire in the fire pit at the camp house as he sped along. Doc and Jake could see him coming on pretty fast. Bobby was on his feet and he muttered a low "Oh shit," to himself.

"What did you say?" asked Jake.

"I said oh shit. I told those boys not to come back unless they were bleeding, snake bit, or dead or else the bet was off,"

"What bet?"

"I bet them a hundred bucks they wouldn't stay out there for two nights. I didn't think they would because I filled their heads with a bunch of spook stories first."

Sport sped into the yard on the four wheeler and he was hysterical."The medicine got him Uncle Bobby. It got him."

"What's he talking about…medicine man? Bobby, what's he talking about?" asked Jake.

"What happened Sport? What happened?" asked Bobby ignoring Jake and putting his arm around Sports shoulder in an attempt to calm him. Sport started crying at that point something none of the men had ever seen. He was shaking like he had the chills.

"We…we were," and he stopped and sobbed some more. Then as quickly as he started he reached down deep and got control of his emotions. He looked Bobby and Jake square in the eyes. "We went back out to find the armadillo that we ran across last night. We found him sniffing his way along the same spot. He almost walked into us but the he smelled us and took off. I went straight after him and Adam made sort of a circle around to the left. Adam ran off the side of the mound and that's when I heard him scream," said Sport with his lip quivering.

"What then?" asked Doc who had been silent to that point.

"Well, I heard him scream and when I looked over to where it came from I saw those red eyes standing high in the air. It scared me bad. I had the rifle and I calmed myself down and I shot it right between the eyes. I know that I hit him 'cause I heard him holler and he started flopping around or jumping."

"So you're telling me you shot something that you think was a 'medicine man' between the eyes and he had Adam caught?" asked Doc.

"Well…yeah, that's what happened," said Sport.

"Did you kill him?"

"I don't know. All I know is that I hit him and then Adam hollered for me to go get Jake so I left and came here as fast as I could."

Chapter 7

At the site Hole struggled to get his bearings. He knew that he had been shot but he didn't know how bad it was. His head hurt for sure but he didn't lose consciousness. The blood was coming out of the wound at a slow trickle and he had to keep wiping it off. It was difficult especially with Adam struggling to get away. He had Adam tied pretty good but his feet were still free and he bounced and kicked Hole in the shins and knees every chance he got. Hole finally figured out that he could force Adam to walk in front of him and avoid most of his foot work.

They got back to the drag line and Hole started to call for Jimmy. After the third time he yelled Jimmy appeared from the other side of the machine in the dark after having snuck back so Hole wouldn't know where he came from.

"What in the hell have you gone and done now? Who is this kid?" bellowed Junior. "Who are you boy and why are you out here?"

"I could ask you the same question and if I were you I would let me go now 'cause my mom's friend and his friends are going to kick your asses when they get here."

"What are you talking about? There ain't nobody around for miles, you just talkin' a load of crap," said Junior. "By the way ass Hole, what happened to your head?"

"I got shot," said Hole.

"We gotta' get the hell outt'a here now," said Junior. They went over to the tent dragging Adam the entire way. Junior started throwing things in bags. Maps, tools, things that might have finger prints on them all got stuffed into canvas bags. He grabbed the last of the water they had and the cooler and they dragged it all out into the open next to the drag line. Junior went over to Donny's camp trailer and opened the door cautiously. He picked up the keys to Donny's truck and tossed them in the grass in front of the door.

"This is going to be fun when we get caught. Kidnapping, grave robbing, how does forty to life sound to you Hole?" Hole just stared back. His head was throbbing badly and tricky questions were not something he could deal with at the time.

"They threw everything in the back of the truck. There was one bag that Junior was especially careful with and he took pains to set it down gently and protect it with anything soft he could find. They tied Adam's feet securely and put him in the middle of the truck seat and headed north. In the dark the giant pot holes in the road were even more deceptive. The bumps seemed harder, the holes deeper, and the progress slower now that they were in a hurry. With Donny passed out in his trailer the lone pickup had no reference in the dark to guide them out like when they arrived in the daylight. It seemed to take forever to cover just one mile not to mention twenty.

At the ranch camp Doc and Jake talked with Bobby about what they knew so far.

"What the hell is the boy talking about?" asked Doc.

"Well, I sort of made up this story about Indian medicine men. They wanted to get scared by a story that might have some truth to it. I told them that the Key Marco Cat effigy was a 'wampus cat'.

"What kind of cat?" asked Doc.

"A wampus cat. There are some stories from a lot of tribes about a woman who looks like a panther that follows people around. I elaborated a little."

"Sounds like you elaborated a lot you old coot," said Jake. "How about the medicine man?"

"Well part of what I told them was true because the Spaniards wrote it down. That's the kind of story they wanted to hear. I stretched it a little too. I told them that he stills wanders the Earth looking for the wampus cat and that they better keep an eye out if they camped on that old village site."

Doc walked over to where Sport was sitting with his mom. Doc's sister looked up at him with tears in her eyes. Jenny was hysterical and Jake was doing his best to calm her.

"Sport, why do you think it was a medicine man like the one Bobby tried to scare you with?"

"Cause he had beady red eyes. They were close together and they shined red. They were also about six feet off the ground just like Bobby said they would be," said Sport.

Doc walked over to the back of the jeep and motioned for Jake to come over.

"There's someone else out there. We need to move now and see if we can find him. The only person that is there for sure is that guy running the drag line but he has been around for weeks if not months," said Doc.

"Okay, let's go," said Jake. He went into the house and got his shotgun and put it in the jeep.

"Jake and I are going out to where Sport last saw Adam. Adam, you're going too. The rest of you need to stay here in case we need something or we find something. That includes you Bobby. Sit tight right here and we'll call you on the radio if we need to get in touch," said Doc as he stashed his old lever action .30/.30 in between the seats. Jenny was frantic. She gave Jake a kiss and told him to be careful. Doc topped off the tank of the jeep from a drum at the barn on his way out and before too long the tail lights were out of sight.

Doc turned off the headlights and drove slowly out to the hammock where the boys had set up camp. He crept forward in the dark stopping every now and then to listen and look. The air was clear and the lights from the coast cast a glow on the eastern horizon. It was quiet except for the occasional whippoorwill and owl calls in the Night. "Nothing, absolutely nothing," whispered Doc.

"What are you thinking?" asked Jake.

"I don't know what to think but I do know we better come up with answers or the girls aren't going to hang around camp very long."

They eased the old Jeep along and finally shut it down when they got to the boys camp. Jake got out first and put a small dim headlight on his head and inspected his old Winchester .30/.30. Doc did the same thing but instead of a rifle he reached in the back of the Jeep for his 12 gauge. They walked around looking at the ground and everything seemed pretty much normal. Nothing had been disturbed beyond what a couple have kids would have done over the course of a camp out.

"Over here," said Jake pointing to a spot on the ground that had been disturbed by the fleeing armadillo. They cast their dim beams around and found where the boys had split up in their pursuit. Jake was on Sport's trail. Eventually Doc had located what he thought was the path that Adam took. They walked slowly and methodically only taking their eyes off the ground to get their bearings and avoid low hanging branches and spider webs. "Look here," said Jake returning to a full standing position.

Doc walked over and saw that Jake had the hull of a .22 short pinched between his thumb and forefinger.

Doc looked down range of where the boy had likely shot and took off in a trot. He nearly fell into the excavation that Hole had been working on. He saw signs of a scuffle and two sets of foot prints. Doc whistled for Jake who came running over to see what Doc had found. They trained both of their lights in the hole. The ground was disturbed from the digging. White sand with long dark roots of the Sable Palm protruding out of the freshly cut sides of the hole shown back at them. There were two sets of footprints in the hole, one much smaller than the other and there was blood everywhere. The men just looked at each other and felt their own blood rush out of their heads as they considered whose blood it might have been.

"Sport must have nailed him," said Doc as he tried to put Jake's mind at ease.

"Hope so," said Jake. "But what if he missed?"

"You know better than that Jake. You've seen him shoot, you've said it before that if you ever got in a gun fight you would want Sport on your side."

"Okay. So he hit the bastard, then what? Didn't kill him. If he'd a had this Model 94 it would have been all over and we would have Adam and the cops could sort it out," said Jake.

"We'll find him. We need to stay calm and think," said Doc. He was looking down sweeping his light and following the tracks out of the woods and onto the canal bank.

The two men picked up the pace and headed north until they could make out the outline of the camp trailer with Donny Gillis rolling around in his own vomit inside. There was one twelve volt light hanging from a wire that was powered by a car battery that had seen better days. As Doc and Jake approached the trailer they slowed their pace, stopping to listen and look. They quietly slipped up to the windows on the south side and looked in. They could see Donny breathing. He was a filthy mess covered with vomit and grease from the evening meal that he wasted all over his home. Doc eased up to the rickety door and tested it quietly. Jake walked around the vehicle. He pulled the hammer back on his Model 94 and fired a round into the marl soil right next to the side of the trailer. The rifle boomed and for an instant the thin aluminum walls of the trailer flexed as if it had taken a short breath. Donny rolled over and pissed his pants adding to the wet greasy stinking mess he already was. He fluttered his eyes in the anemic light from the bulb. In that moment, Doc put his shoulder into the door and it came open. He had the barrel of the shotgun in Donny's nose before Donny could process anything in his infused brain.

"Where is he?" asked Doc and he gave the shotgun a little shove. A trickle of blood rand out of Donny's left nostril.

"Where is who? Where is who?" questioned Donny as he tried to turn his head away from the curiously warm barrel of the gun not realizing that it was his own blood that warmed the barrel.

"Who else is here?" asked Jake.

"There ain't nobody else here but me. Been like that for months. Hey, ain't you boys from the ranch next door?"

Jake put his boot in Donny's chest and gave him a shove.

"Now," said Jake, "who else is out here?"

"Nobody I reckon. A coupla' friends of mine come out for supper. We drank a lot, grilled some meat. If they ain't out there they must be gone. Probably went back to town."

"Who are they? What are their names?" asked Jake while Doc looked around the little trailer.

"I don't know."

Doc rapped him on top of the head with the plug end of a heavy duty extension cord.

"Hey, that hurts," moaned Donny.

"You haven't seen anything yet. Who are

they, where are they?" asked Jake again.

Jake had Donny's middle fingernail squeezed tight under a .30/.30 cartridge. He started to squirm, then whimper as Jake increased the pressure.

"Alright, alright. The guy I know is named Junior. That's all I know. Met him at a flea market about five years ago in Ft. Lauderdale. I don't know the other one. Junior called him 'hole', that's all I know."

"They came all the way out here for a barbeque?"

"Well sort of. Junior came out for that and to look at some fossils I found. He wanted to look for some himself too. Wanted to drink and cook out also. I think I did most of the drinking though by the looks of it," said Donny.

"You collect rocks Donny?" asked Doc.

"I love to collect fossils, not rocks. It's what's left over from prehistoric animals if the conditions are just right. Down here the conditions are just right everywhere."

"I know what fossils are," said Doc. "What do you do with them?"

"I sell a few every now and then. That's how I met Junior, up at that flea market. I don't go to flea markets much anymore. The people who buy my stuff know how to reach me. That's how I bought my screened porch last year."

"What does Junior buy?"

"He was down here to look. He seems to like mastodon teeth, and the giant sharks teeth."

"What does he like to sell?"

"I don't really know. When I first run into him he had a velvet thing that rolled up. It was full of arrow heads or something. All laid in there in their own little pockets so they wouldn't bump into each other."

"Anything else?"

"Not that I seen. He had a tooth that looked like the last one they pulled out of my head when I went to the dentist. It had a hole drilled through it and he wore it around his neck on a leather necklace with a couple of beads about the size of buckshot on either side of it. I remember asking him about it, I asked him what he would take for it and he just looked at me and grinned. He never said anything about it. The next day it was gone."

"What's he look like?" asked Doc.

"He's a big dude, kinda' redneck lookin'. Every time I ever seen him he's wearing a cowboy hat with a western shirt with the sleeves cut off. I reckon he'd go about six one, maybe two hunnerd, maybe fifty years old. His hair sticks out under the back of his hat and he usually has a coupla' days of whiskers."

"What about the other one? What did you call him? Hole"?

"Yep, that's what Junior called him. He don't talk much. He's about as big as a Sasquatch and likely smells worse than one. The dude looks like some kind of a monster, like Frankenstein. I mean he looks put together. His hands don't look like they belong on his body, they're huge like a tennis racket head. He's got long arms too and his skull looks too small for his body. He's just real big too. He stays dirty all the time like he's been digging in the dirt. It makes him look just that much worse than most."

"So what's the deal? When did they come out here?" asked Doc.

"This morning, or yesterday, I don't know. I don't know what time it is or what day it is. They came out and puttered around all afternoon while I ran the dragline. They picked up some shells, a couple of pieces of antler and some other stuff. Then we cooked supper and I got drunk."

"Did you see any kids out here?"

"Nope, no kids. I don't ever see no one out here."

"What were they driving?"

"Three quarter ton Ford four wheel drive truck with a camper top on it. It was brown with big tires on it. It was dirty too. Everything gets dirty driving out here."

"Get up and get yourself cleaned up. We're going for a ride," said Doc.

"It's four in the morning, can't we just wait until daylight?" pleaded Donny.

"I said get up and get cleaned up."

Donny thought to himself that his head felt like a hand grenade went off inside of it. He was nauseated and his throat burned and the stench of his own body made him sick. He found a clean towel and some clothes and staggered outside and around the back side of the trailer where he had affixed a shower head so he could stand up and take a shower. He hated the little shower and toilet combination bathroom inside the trailer because you really couldn't sit or stand and be comfortable. He groaned in the dark as the cold weak stream trickled out of the shower head. He was sore from lying contorted on the floor; the cold water did nothing to alleviate the stiffness in his neck and the pain in his arm.

"I'm going back to the camp house to get the truck and a few supplies," said Jake as he and Doc stood outside the little trailer in the dark. Each of them silently put together different scenarios in their heads about what could have happened a few hours earlier. They both knew that soon they would be faced with making a decision if they hoped to get Adam back. They still didn't have a clue about what they were dealing with but they knew more now than they did two hours ago.

"Is there anything you want me get and bring?"

"Yeah, get my lasso, the old soft one, it's hanging in the horse trailer. Better get a phone and a couple of the hand held radios and some extra clothes. My wallet and money is in a dry box behind the seat, just make sure it's there and I didn't leave it in the house."

"Okay. I'm going to move, I should be back here in about an hour if I don't get slowed down at the house. Keep an eye on this loser. I don't really think he will give you a hard time and if he does it won't be a problem for you to handle,"

"Will do," said Doc.

Jake started the Jeep up, backed away from the trailer and vanished in the dark.

Chapter 8

Junior Davis finally hit the asphalt about three hours after he left Donny's trailer. Heavy fog had rolled in from the Gulf. Not being able to move very fast under the best of conditions was a given. Adding the fog to the journey through the immense pot holes made the trip torturous.

U.S. Highway 27 seemed quiet in the fog but Junior knew that the blanket masked the dangerous truck traffic that was surely lurking up and down this infamous and deadly stretch of road. Sugarcane trucks were underway to the fields. The sugar trains were creaking across miles of tracks and bad road crossings where warning signals only worked sometimes. He hit the northbound lane and floored the truck. He was careful not to drive too fast because he was painfully aware that the stretch of road he was driving on was a favorite hunting ground for local law enforcement. He had Lee county tags on his truck that immediately identified him as an outsider who would eagerly pay the fine before facing the long trip back out to the Glades to go to traffic court. He had the window cracked to help evacuate some of the cigarette smoke that was filling the cab and to get rid of some of the stink from Hole. Adam fidgeted on the seat and if it got too pronounced or annoying, Hole would clamp down with one of his ham sized hands on the top of a thigh and Adam would make himself still again. It was dark in the cab except for the dash light which did little to illuminate anything. The air rushing in the window was cold but at least it was fresh. Adam prayed that Junior didn't decide to put the window up and turn on the heater. He thought to himself that would surely make him gag.

Once they passed Palmdale Junior accelerated the truck. The fog was patchy now and driving had the feel of flying through broken clouds. Junior drove on. He still didn't have a good idea of what had happened back out at the site and especially how he wound up with this kid in his truck. His mind raced between the immediate situation and thoughts of what happens to people who kidnap others whether planned or not. He knew Hole would be no help when it came to complex reasoning so he didn't bother to even formulate anything but the simplest concrete questions.

"What happened?" asked Junior. "Go real slow, from the start."

"Well, I left the trailer and started walking and follerin' the map that…"

"I know that you dumbass. What happened when you crossed paths with this kid?"

"Well, I was digging. There is lots of material out there. I got caught up in the stuff that was coming out of the hole, you know, looking down a lot and strainin' to see with the little headlight and the red lenses."

"Okay, then what happened?"

"Well, I was down in the hole shoveling and looking when I heard this commotion coming through the woods. I figgerd it was a coupla' hogs or somethin' so I just set there quiet to wait and see what happened. I stood up and seen this armadillo peel off to the left of me and then the next thing this kid came barrelin' in on top of me. He knocked me back and once I got my feet back under me I stood up and pow! I got shot between the eyes I figger."

"Yeah that's right!" said Adam, "and if Sport had the magnum we wouldn't have been having this talk right now."

"Shut up kid," said Junior as Hole clamped back down on Adam's thigh.

"So there was another one?"

"I tried to tell you back at Donny's but you were in such a hurry I didn't get a chance."

"Hole, that was important. They're probably looking for us right now, every law enforcement agency in the state. Not only were we poaching grave sites on private land in the company of a drunk state employee, now we are kidnappers. Do you see a problem with this? Why didn't you leave the kid?"

"Why didn't you? You were the one in such a big hurry. And yes, I do see the problem with this," said Hole.

"Who is the other one? Where is he?"

"He's my best friend and he probably went back to the camp house to tell our uncles and aunts and the rest of the family that you took me," said Adam frantically.

"Pipe down kid or I'm throwin' you out the window. What family? What's their name and what camp house are you talking about?"

Adam sat in silence and considered what too much information might spell for him. At that moment he decided that if he couldn't physically control his situation he could possibly control it with information.

"What family?" yelled Junior. It was met

with more silence.

"You know that my family knows the Governor," said Adam after ten minutes of silence.

Junior and Hole just looked at each other."Yeah and I'm a monkey's uncle," said Junior.

"He's at the camp. Came for the roundup," said Adam, then silence. Daylight had begun to filter into the cab of the truck. Adam looked straight ahead for a long time. Finally he couldn't stand it any longer and he looked at Hole. He wasn't prepared for what he saw. Neither was Junior for that matter. Hole's forehead had a bullet hole in it. From where the bullet hit there were four cuts that radiated out in a cross pattern. One little diamond shaped piece of skin flapped whenever he moved his head and you could see pink tissue under it whenever it moved. The entire area was black and blue and encrusted with blood. Both of his eyes were blackened from the impact of the little round. They were swollen almost to the point of being closed. There were dried rivulets of blood from where it had coursed down his face and there were other areas where it had been smeared. The blood added a new layer of stink, the wet metallic smell of too much blood in the air. His shirt was filthy from digging and sweating and it had blood all over it too. Hole didn't seem to notice and the only bothersome thing to him was that his vision was compromised to the point that he could barely see out of his eyes.

To Adam he was a monster incarnate. He looked gruesome and it scared him to know that he was sitting next to him. He grew pale and shaky when he thought that this is what caught him in the dark and held him. He thought to himself that he was glad that Sport shot him and he wished he would have shot him again and again so he wouldn't have to be enduring this right now. He thought about his mom and Sport and he worried about Jake, Doc, and Uncle Bobby. He regained some of his composure with the reassuring thought that all of these people and more would be looking for him and he would be found.

"Damn son, you look rough," said Junior once he got a good look at Hole.

"I feel okay 'cept I can't see all that good."

"When I get a chance we'll get some ice on that head and we'll see if it helps the swelling," said Junior.

"Okay, that would be good," said Hole.

Jake rolled into camp just as the sky to the east had begun to lighten. There was a roaring fire in the fire pit. Jenny ran out to the Jeep hoping to find Adam safe. When she saw that Jake was alone she fought back the tears. Jake could tell she had been crying for a long time but he could also see that she had fought through it with the same resolve that had attracted him in the first place. She was indeed distraught but now she was mad and he could sense it. She was determined now more than ever to find her son and would stop at nothing to do just that.

"What did you find out?" asked Jenny.

"Not too much. There were a couple of

106

guys staying out there with the dragline operator form the state. He said they were fossil hunters but there is probably more to it than that. They probably got Adam. There are two of them. Sport shot one of them during some sort of altercation. The likely reacted and grabbed Adam because he couldn't think of anything else to do. I don't have a strong feeling that they would hurt him. Sounds like just a couple of stupid rednecks that got in a situation. We'll find him."

"I know. I feel a little better since I got to see you. It's been a little crazy around here all night," she said.

"Where is Bobby?"

"He left a couple of hours ago. He feels terrible because this whole thing, this camp out and the ghost stories were his idea. He bet the boys they wouldn't camp out there."

"What do you mean?"

"I mean he bet them. Het bet money."

"Damn him too. Now I gotta' worry about what he is teaching my nephew and his friends on top everything else."

"He feels really bad. Don't go too hard on him. It was in fun and if he had even the slightest idea that this could have happened out here of all places he would have never done it. He loves both of them like they are his, just like he loves you and Doc."

"Well, I can't worry about it now. Did he say where he was going?"

"Not really, he just took off. He has his phone."

Jake gathered the items that Doc asked to bring and put them into the truck. Sport came out and watched him for a few minutes before asking if he could go too.

"What's on your mind buddy?"

"Lots of stuff, said Sport, "Adam mostly and that dude I shot at."

"Well, if it is any consolation, you nailed him. Right between the headlights," said Jake.

"How did he get away then, how come he was able to get away with Adam if I hit him?"

"The guy is built like a cave man. I imagine his skull is pretty thick. Besides, Bobby gave you a single shot twenty two rifle with short rounds. I found the hull, it was a long shot. I imagine he has a pretty good headache this morning but that's probably about it."

"Can I go with you to find Adam?"

"You need to stay here with your mom and dad. It helps Aunt Jenny too, knowing that you are okay. Besides, if Adam got away he will come back here. I need for you to be on the lookout for him. I want you get a couple of the horses tuned up today and beyond anything I want you to promise that you will stay away from where this happened last night. Promise?"

"Okay," said Sport. "Promise."

Chapter 9

Jake returned to Donny's place a little over an hour and a half after he left it. Donny looked a little better than he did earlier. At least he was clean and didn't reek of vomit and urine. The sun on his head felt good to him and reassured him that he would once again feel better as time passed. It had been nearly nine hours since the ordeal when Adam was abducted and Hole bought himself a twenty two short round between the eyes.

"What now?" asked Jake when he saw Doc.

"Don't really know. I see where they drove off, I guess we might as well just follow as far as we go until we come up with something better," said Doc.

"What do we do with your sidekick?" asked Jake.

"I don't think we have any choice other than bring him along. He may be useful, for something, Not sure for what but something."

"Donny, come over here. We need to talk. My fiancé's boy was taken by your friends last night. You are going with us to try and find him. Don't get any ideas like you have been kidnapped or taken against your will because you are in enough trouble already. Enough to send you to jail for a long time. If you try anything stupid you'll wish that you were going to jail because we can bury you in a thousand places that no one will ever find."

"Listen fellas, I don't want no trouble from no one. I'm just a flunky dragline operator for the state out here tryin' to make a livin'. I pick up a few bones and fossils here and there to make a little extra. If I can help I will but I ain't do nothing to hurt myself or put myself at risk of going to jail. I don't know those guys well but I can spot them and I am willing to help."

"Let's keep it that way," said Jake.

The three men picked their way across miles of potholes and after about an hour of calling Jake finally contacted Bobby.

"Where did you get off to?" asked Jake.

"I couldn't stand it any longer, you know, sitting around the camp house with everyone speculating. I had a hunch that whoever took Adam had to come out at some time on the north end of the canal road. I drove out there. Where are you guys?"

"We're about thirty or forty minutes from the hard road. You?"

"Not too far from where you guys. I'll meet you at the end of the canal road. Jake, there were fresh muddy tracks where they hit the pavement. Big mud grip tracks, it had to be them, there is no one else out there. The hit the highway and headed north," said Bobby.

"They're in a four wheel drive pickup. It's brown with big mud tires on it. There are two of them and they have Adam. The truck is brown," said Jake.

"I'll be waiting for you," said Bobby.

"Bobby, we have someone with us. The dragline operator. He filled us in with the details we know so far."

"Okay, we can deal with him. Think he is telling the truth?"

"I think so, he doesn't have anything to

gain by not telling the truth."

Jake, Doc, and Donny crawled along over the treacherous road for what seemed forever. They closed the last mile to the hard road and as they approached they could see Bobby pacing around waiting for them. When they were finally there Jake and Doc got out of the truck first. They walked over to Bobby. Donny could see them talking quietly to each other when Doc turned around and motioned for Donny to get out and join them. Donny walked over, his head still pounding. He squinted his eyes in the blinding sun and extended his had to Bobby who refused it. Bobby turned his back slightly to Donny and then without warning gave him a roundhouse backhand across the side of his head. Donny was stunned by the blow that just added another layer of agony to his already aching head.

"Whoa, whoa there Uncle Bobby. Take it easy," said Jake as he held Bobby's arm in anticipation of another blow.

"That was a warning shot. If I find out you had anything to do with that boys disappearance there won't be enough of you left for the buzzards to find," said Bobby.

"Mister I ain't got a dog in this fight. I want to help you find that boy. I promise," said Donny.

Bobby put his hand on the nape of Donny's neck and squeezed. Donny cowered and prepared himself as best he could for he figured was going to be another wallop, perhaps to the face this time.

"Come over here with me," said Bobby as he pulled Donny along to the front of his truck. "I want to hear the whole story from the start."

Doc and Jake looked on from a distance. After about thirty minutes Bobby and Donny rejoined them. Donny was quiet and looked a little paler then he did before Bobby had his talk with him. His hangover already made him look sick and pasty, now he just looked a little worse.

"I'm going to take Donny with me," said Bobby. "You guys stay here until I call you. I've got some business to take care of out at the field office. If you want, wait here or head into town, maybe you can come up with something there. Just don't get too far off."

"Okay, we might ride over to the campground where Donny was staying and see if we can't find out anything about Junior and Hole," said Jake.

"…and Jake, please be discreet. We don't need anybody else in on this until we find out more about what has happened," said Bobby.

Bobby turned his truck around and headed back to a long access road that would eventually take him far out into a sugar cane field to a remote barn that served as a mechanics station, office, fuel depot, helicopter pad, and communications link for the Pan Caribbean sugar consortium for whom Bobby now worked. When he started working in the sugar business is was a tightly held family operation. It was gradually gobbled up by Pan Caribbean. He had worked as a laborer until eventually he became an electrician. With just five more years until retirement Bobby had worked his way up through the ranks. He stayed up to speed with technology and eventually found himself not only the lead electrician but he also took care of telemetry equipment, pumps, generators and a whole host of other things that kept this modern operation thriving in a world market that to him has gone 'nuts'. He was glad he was retiring in the near future for many reasons not the least of which was the price of sugar globally. He wondered how long the American people would tolerate their taxes artificially propping up the price just because of a communist takeover of Cuba a half century ago. It didn't make much sense to him but he had a good job. It had surely lost the appeal of a family run business but with it came other perks. He got to travel some to the operations in Central America and to Honduras a couple of times a year. He always tacked on a couple of extra days for fishing. Pan Caribbean had a couple of very nice boats tucked away at these ports of call which any of the crew could use when they visited.

"Where are we going?" asked Donny.

"I need to stop by the office and pick up a couple of things. You don't need to worry about it."

"Damn, I thought I worked out in the middle of nowhere. At least I get to see trees and water," said Donny who looked out over the endless sea of green that stretched to the horizon in all directions. In the distance he could see a large cloud of smoke towering into the clear blue sky. The air was still and to him it reminded of pictures his father brought back from Vietnam after a B-52 strike. He knew it was the sugar fields being burned of their leaves. Soon the

113

mechanical harvesters would follow as would the trucks and the trains.

"When I first started working for this outfit we farmed about seven thousand acres right around the mill. We have fifty thousand under cultivation now and it's fifty miles to the mill from our furthest field," said Bobby.

"You've seen lots of changes," said Donny.

Bobby just looked at him and didn't say anything. The conversation was over. Bobby pulled into the parking area and stopped the truck. He took the keys out of the ignition.

"Don't get any stupid ideas. You will never make it out of here on foot."Bobby got out of the truck and walked up to the entrance door, put a key in the lock and went in. He worked fast to gather the things he thought he needed. He picked up a pair of two way radios, extra batteries and a charger. He reached into his desk and retrieved his spare 1911 Colt and two boxes of ammo. He went into the break room and stuffed a bag with crackers, cookies, and a couple of candy bars and he was done. He went back out to the truck headed back out the way he came in. Every ten minutes or so he would try and call Doc and Jake on his cell phone but he was still too far from a tower. After about an hour Jake answered.

"Jake, listen. I have a plan," said Bobby.

"Okay, shoot."

"I need to tell you in person, things being the way they are these days I don't really trust these phones. I am about thirty five minutes from the highway. I want you and Doc to meet me at the truck stop south of Palmdale. Rio's Truck Stop. I should be up there in about an hour or so. If I am going to be late I will call you," said Bobby.

"Okay," said Jake and he ended the call.

"What did say?" asked Jake.

"He's hatched some sort of a plan. He didn't say what it was but he wanted to tell us in person, not over the phone. We're going to meet him at Rio's in about an hour or so."

Chapter 10

Four and a half hours before Jake and Doc arrived at Rio's Truck Stop, Junior was just leaving. He had stopped in to refuel, use the bathroom and buy a few items. Things had been fairly quiet and he wasn't sure that anyone even knew that they had the kid or what had taken place back at the site. He was getting fairly comfortable with the idea that things were quiet even though he admitted to himself that he didn't have a clue about what was going on behind him. He did notice that the gunshot wound that hole has sustained had gotten much worse. The swelling was grotesque and even Hole had started to complain a little bit.

"I'm pull in here and see if I can't get you something that may make you feel a little better," said Junior. Hole just looked in his direction and nodded. Junior went in the store, paid for his gas and bought a few food items, some beer, and a bag of ice. Hole still had his relentless grip on Adam's thigh. Junior opened the tailgate and the rear window of the camper and poured the ice into a cooler. He packed a quart sized plastic zip bag with ice. His first aid get caught the cornier of his eye and he retrieved it as well. He came around and got back in the truck.

"Here," said Junior. Put this on you head, it will help the swelling. Junior doused a clean bandage with hydrogen peroxide and put it in Hole's hand and then directed up to the wound. He couldn't really tell but hole seemed to wince a little. Junior gave him a couple of pain killers and a cold beer. Hole smiled at the sound of the beer opening. He put the ice pack against his swollen face and relaxed his grip on Adam a little.

"Mister, I hope you head starts to feel better. I don't like you and you're going to be in a whole lot of trouble but I kinda' feel bad that your face and head are so messed up," said Adam. Adam really didn't know what to think other than if he got the chance he was going to run.

When they made it north of Palmdale without any interference, Junior called Jimmy.

"Jimmy, it's Junior."

"Hey man, how are things? What did you find out at your buddy's canal bank?"

"Jimmy we can talk about that later. There was lots of material, let's just leave it at that," said Junior.

"What the hell is that supposed to mean?"

"Jimmy, we got a problem and it ain't no small problem."

"What's going on? Is it the law? Did you guys get caught because if you did this conversation is over," said Jimmy.

"It ain't the law yet. But I would expect that to change pretty soon."

"Okay, spill it, what's going on?"

"Everything was going fine. We got my buddy drunk off his ass and he passed out so no worries there. We went out to dig. I went one way, Hole went the other. Apparently there was a coupla' kids from the adjoining ranch camping out and they surprised Hole while he was diggin'. One of them shot him in the head," said Junior.

117

"What happened to the other one, you said there were a couple of kids, how many were there?"

"Two, as near as we can tell. The other one is sitting here beside me."

"What the hell are you talking about man? Why is the other kid with you?"

"Hole caught him after the other one shot him in the head. He brought him back up to Donny's trailer. I didn't know what to do with him. I'd a felt bad if I had left him out there to fend for himself and try to get back to where he came from in the dark. So we took him."

"You took him. You didn't take him. These days it is called kidnap and if you think going to jail over a few Indian bones was inconvenient, your ass will get buried for the rest of your life if you get caught this time."

Junior pulled off on a small dirt side road and turned the engine off. He walked around to the front of his truck.

"Then just what in the hell do you propose I do? Do you want me to kill him and feed him to the gators?"

"No don't kill anybody you dumbass. I can't believe you just said that. I need time to think. I need time to think about what you and Hole have done and what I have to do to get you out of this before anyone associates me with it. Where are you now?"

"We are just barely past Palmdale heading north on twenty seven."

"Did anyone see you?"

"Nope. Donny was passed out. I reckon the other kid made it back to where he came

118

from. I heard an ATV start up about an hour after Hole got shot. That's when we left. I imagine he went back and told his story. The only thing out there is the Widon family ranch. They have a bunkhouse out there for the cowboys. I wouldn't have any idea who might be in there now. Probably some hunters this time of year."

"Okay, here is what I want you to do. Keep heading north. When you get to Lake Wales I want you to take road 60 and drive east. You are going to cross the Kissimmee River. Keep going, this is important. Not too far after you cross the river you will come to another road that runs north and south, its highway 441. Go left there and just keep on going until you can't go any further. When you stop, go right. The next river you come to is the Saint Johns. There is a bridge over the river and a boat ramp. Take the access road to the boat ramp. There is a little store down there. I want you to hang out there until someone comes to get you. Call me when you get there. Do something with your truck, hide it if you can.

"You the boss. I hope you know what you are doing," said Junior and hung up. Junior repacked the bag of ice and handed the fresh pack to Hole who immediately placed it on his head and they headed north.

Chapter 11

Jimmy Goodland had just spent the last thirty or so hours piecing together evidence of what was beginning to look like the mother lode of all pre-Columbian sites in the Sunshine state. It was not just a site as most people would think. It was series of villages linked together in a long chain of villages that spanned nearly a hundred miles along the St. Johns River. The people who had inhabited the area were collectively lumped together and were euphemistically called the St. Johns Culture. They didn't get the same historical press that the Indians in the southwest part of the state did because their sites were far removed from development for a long time. Even when things did start showing up, no one put the pieces together. It was a fairly modern revelation that their culture was much more akin to a city state type of arrangement versus random villages along a large and productive waterway. The villagers there were protected somewhat from the Spanish intrusion because they lived in the foreboding interior. The Spanish were content to sail around the coast of the state for many years building forts and missions without venturing too far into the interior. Although Spanish contact was probably rare for these people it is highly likely that they were actually the first people on the continent who encountered a white man. Jimmy Goodland felt strongly about this notion. So strong that he spent two days last year arguing with the tourism development board in St. Augustine about where Ponce de Leon actually landed.

"This is a ruse predicated on old stories

and hearsay," Goodland would tell the council. "I implore you all to change your brochures and your advertising so people don't get misled. There is no fountain of youth. Juan Ponce did not land here," he would say as he recounted over and over the evidence he had. It fell on deaf ears. If the town fathers actually thought that what he said would affect tourism he might have been able to gain some ground. No one goes to St. Augustine because of the thought that Ponce de Leon may have first set foot there. They come for the cheap motels, the beach, and the tourist money grab joints all up and down St. George Street not to mention the cheap food and warm weather.

Yesterday in a posh hotel room at Tampa's Bayfront area Jimmy met with a pair of heavy hitter antiquities dealers from New York. They had heard of Jimmy in the circles they travelled in and they knew his reputation for producing very valuable items that he collected from around the state. The secret meeting had been arranged through one of Jimmy's clients. At first Jimmy was reluctant to meet anyone and was happy to keep things the way they were. Negotiations went on for nearly a year before Jimmy agreed to meet the men. He didn't know much about them except that they both had lots of money and they liked to spend it on expensive pre-Columbian items that came from Florida. In particular, grave goods and human remains. Jimmy understood the grave goods thing but he couldn't for the life if him understand why anyone would want old human bones. For Jimmy, bones were something that got in the way. They were simply tossed aside. If anything, once he or any of his diggers started hitting bones and teeth it simply meant that they were getting close to the real treasure, the intact pots that many tribes buried their dead with.

"Not bones Jimmy. Intact skeletons. All the bones. I have developed a certain clientele that likes intact skeletons," said one of the men.

"What do they do with them?" asked Jimmy.

"I don't know. I don't care. Maybe they keep them in their closets," the man said with a laugh. "They pay handsomely for them."

"How much?"

"I won't say but I can tell you that if you bring me an intact skeleton with perfect teeth I can assure you that you will earn at least twenty thousand dollars for it."

Jimmy did the math and his mind raced across hundreds of sites where he had been before. Sites that he ransacked back in his younger days. Sites where he scattered bones like toothpicks just to get at the pots. He had been earning upwards of ten thousand dollars for a good pot for several years. He had earned a hefty twenty five thousand from a perfect effigy pot that he had found at a timber company site in the panhandle. He thought to himself that he could double his money if he slowed down long enough to collect the bones from the owners of the pots.

"What is it that you think I can do for you?" asked Jimmy.

"We had a steady supply of material up until two years ago," said the other man intently.

"Steady supply? I'd like to hear more about that," said Jimmy who considered himself one of the best. He had never heard of anything begin steady or reliable in this business.

"That's right. Steady. Our man worked for the state for many years then things started to get a little screwy with him. He was eccentric to begin with then he went off the deep end. He got fired from the state for some of his activity on the side. Nothing illegal, it just didn't sit well with some of the politicians. He stopped a couple of really big developments from ever getting started. They tried to pay him off but he wouldn't hear of it."

"So then what happened?" asked Jimmy.

"When he lost his job he had to do something for money. That's how we met him. Two years ago he caught his wife fooling around with a judge from Sable County. He left her and moved south. Two weeks after he moved they found her body in a dumpster along I-10 with nine bullet holes in her."

"And they think he did it," said Jimmy.

"Of course they do. So happens the judge was married at the time but no one has ever purposed the idea that he may have been the one that set up the hit," said pot man.

"We think we know where the material came from. We had an analysis done of the soil particles attached to some of the items and compared them to the data base at the University. What we received were artifacts and human remains from the early archaic period in Florida but we didn't have to go as far or as expensive as molecular archaeology. It was there in front of us the whole time in the pottery. The style of pottery is called St. Johns Incised."

Jimmy knew what the man was talking about but he didn't show it. If Jimmy Goodland knew anything, he knew about pottery. He could tell the difference between Swift Creek stamped and Crooked River stamped in the dark just by feel. He swore he could smell Glades Plain pottery. He had seven hundred pounds of Carrabelle punctated and Wakulla check stamped fragments in boxes in his garage.

"So where do you think the material came from?" asked Jimmy.

"We know it came from somewhere along the St. Johns River. Where? Don't know. That's what we need you to find out."

"Tell me more. I can't just stop my life and take off up the river to find some rogue pirate archaeologist."

"We don't want you to do that. We don't think you could find him anyway."

"Just hang on a minute there. I could find that man when no one else could," said Jimmy after taking offense to the last comment.

"That's not what we mean. We don't think he exists anymore. He is gone, disappeared. No evidence at all that he is anywhere to be found."

"So what's the deal? You want me to go up there and try to find where he was digging? Want me to dig? Sorry fellas, I haven't dug a mound in fifteen years. My back and my nerves can't take it," said Jimmy.

"We don't want you to dig up anything."

"Then what?" asked Jimmy again.

"Remember that wreck that was found three years ago between Key West and Havana? All the newspapers wrote about it. They nicknamed it 'La Sangria' supposedly because of the jubilant celebration that happened after the discovery in Key West. The locals chose sangria as the drink of the day."

"Everything is a jubilant celebration in Key West. The last hurricane swept two people off the dock and the party never stopped. Yeah I remember the wreck," said Jimmy.

"Conservative estimates put the value of that wreck at a billion dollars. The state is involved as is the government of Spain," said pot man.

"What does that have to do with the guy you are looking for?" asked Jimmy.

"The owner of the salvage company sent a couple of his cronies up to look for our guy. They had their pockets full of gold bars and emeralds, all sort of stuff from the wreck. They were looking to make a deal with him. Our guy turned them down. Said that gold and jewels can fluctuate with the global economy but pre-Colombian relics never fluctuate. They couldn't understand but the owner sure did. He was willing to trade pure gold bars one to one for burial items but the man wouldn't budge. He told them there was plenty of gold right where he stood. It was like they insulted him. Anyway, this is where they encountered him." The man took out a St. Johns Water Conservation Area map and pointed to the spot.

"You want me to go up there and find gold?" asked Jimmy.

"No. Unfortunately we agree with the same economic principles our archaeologist friend had. We want you to go up there and find where he stashed the stuff. The last year that he was up there he knew that he was going to get tagged for the murder of his wife. He figured he would either beat it or if he did go to jail it would be some sort of symbolic short term thing to keep everyone happy including the judge that was fooling with his wife. He stashed stuff for when he got out of jail."

"Where?" asked Jimmy.

"We're not really sure but we think somewhere around here," said the bone man. "In the trunks of five or six old cars," He added.

"I am still not sure that I follow you. What is it that you want me to do?" asked Jimmy.

"We want you to go up there and find the cars and what is in them. We can pay you a third of what you find. We estimate three hundred thousand dollars. You can keep whatever gold you find to yourself."

"I'm not really in a position to…" The older of the two men broke out a stack of crisp bills totaling twenty thousand dollars.

"This should help you with expenses. Here is our contact information. If you get caught don't call us. If you don't contact us we will find you, I promise," said the pot man.

After leaving Tampa, Jimmy headed east for about an hour thinking out loud to his self about the meeting. He wondered about the implications and mainly about how he could maximize his take in the venture. He knew right

126

off that he wouldn't try to double cross these two. He didn't know them but for the kind of money they were talking about he figured them to be the type who might bury him in fresh concrete if he tried anything. It was an uncomfortable new metric that he wasn't accustomed to. Now he felt like he was on the other side after years of squelching others who tried to put the make on him. It worried him but he figured if he did what they asked of him things should turn out okay.

"There is nothing wrong with a little insurance, just in case," said Jimmy to himself as he picked up his cell phone and dialed.

"Junior, it's me," said Bobby.

"Hey man, where are you?" came the voice on the other end.

"I am heading to the house to pick up some things that we are going to need."

"I want you to call me when you get to the boat landing and update me. Is the kid okay?" asked Jimmy.

"Yeah, he's fine. Getting a little cranky."

"What about Hole?" asked Jimmy.

"Well, I stopped a while back and got him some stuff to clean up his head and some pain medicine. He started putting ice on his head to keep the swellin' down. It looks like it is working but that spot where the bullet hit him is turnin' kinda' white and gray but he ain't complaining about pain no more," said Junior.

"Well, just keep doing what you're doing. Don't let anybody see him if you can help it. Even without a bullet hole in his head he stands out in a crowd if you know what I mean,"

127

said Jimmy.

"I know what you mean, that's how come most of our meetings are at night," chuckled Junior. Hole just stared at him. "We'll call you when we get to the boat landing."

Chapter 12

Jimmy closed his phone up and headed for his house. He lived a few miles south of Kissimmee in an area that used to be pure Florida wilderness before the days of Disney. His house was built by his grandfather from the hearts of magnificent pine trees and over the years had been added on to with pine and rough sawn cypress wood that was harvested nearby. The inside of the house looked like a museum. Jimmy was a master at replicating the technology of ancient Floridians. The walls were hung with all sorts of items that he had made over the years. There were at least a dozen bows, display cases full of arrowheads, spears, swords whose edges were crafted with the teeth of tiger sharks. The mantle of the fireplace was made form an eight foot section of an old dugout canoe that had been sawn in half lengthwise and mounted into the limestone hearth. It had a glass top on it and inside it there was pure white sand with pottery shards scattered in it. Over the mantle hung the head of one of the biggest white tailed deer ever taken in the state. Jimmy liked to talk about the deer when people asked. Most of the time he would spin this long tale about how he took the animal with a bow he made from Live Oak wood with an arrow he made from river cane, tipped with a point that he made himself out of a piece of chert that came from Georgia. Kids were especially in awe as were the occasional adults who would listen to his story about how he had been on the trail of the of the monster buck for three years before he actually stalked him and killed him. It was a good story that stirred deep primal feelings in people who liked that kind of stuff but it didn't happen quite that way. Jimmy had been hunting indeed but not with a bow that he made. He was near the headwaters of the St. Johns River in his boat near the end of hunting season several years ago when he could hear dogs baying in the distance. He maneuvered his jon boat to stay ahead of the baying hounds. He was rewarded when the huge buck blasted out of the cypress trees and into the river. Jimmy only had to pull the boat alongside and cut his throat. Once dispatched, he put the animal into the boat and headed downstream for a couple of miles where he pulled the beast out onto the bank of the river and shot him with his rifle to authenticate his story.

When Jimmy got the buck back to the gas station, pool hall, gun, store, video rental, barbeque and deer processing place known as Lucky's he was an instant celebrity. People stopped their trucks and pulled in to get a look at the deer hanging from a scale off to the side of the building. His picture of him and the deer were plastered everywhere across the state. Jimmy liked the publicity and the story stuck. Jimmy glanced up at the mounted deer head and grinned.

Jimmy's wife was off visiting her sister in Georgia and things were quiet the house. He went back to his office for lack of a better term and dug through a rack full of maps that he had collected over the years. He grabbed a stack of maps that highlighted the area of the St. Johns River that he was most interested in. They included topographical maps, several satellite images filtered to show water course both new and old, and a satellite picture of vegetation patterns throughout the year. His favorite standby however was a fairly recent invention. It was a remarkable thirty by forty inch map taken with an infrared camera and integrated with a radar altimeter. The images from both devices were then combined to produce an image of uncanny accuracy that would show in the minutest detail the subtle differences in elevation across any landscape. Tiny differences down to less than a foot could be discerned. The images weren't widely available because of special licensing requirements but if you knew the right people at NASA or one of the farm managers at one of the big operations down in the Glades, it was easy enough to get your hands on one albeit for a price. Jimmy purchased his for three thousand dollars a couple of years ago in a secret deal with a surveyor who had run into hard times.

Jimmy took down several dusty books that hadn't seen light in years. He thumbed through them and carefully put bookmarks in places that he would come back to later. He carefully studied the drawings of Jacques LeMoyne as if he were going in search of the living people that were depicted in the sixteenth century images. They demonstrated a robust group of well-fed people living along the river. He found it amusing that the Spanish weren't the first people there because they were too busy sailing around the south and west coast looking for the fountain of youth. He kicked back in his chair and whispered to himself, "Rio de

Corientes." He let his mind wander to a time when interlopers to this place paid a heavy price.

He flipped on his laptop computer and thumbed through an anatomy book trying to figure out how many bones an 'intact' human skeleton had He researched how many teeth adult humans had. He was beginning to get an idea just how rare this skeleton would be. Certainly there were many less than perfect ones out there. Jimmy thought about it for a little while and walked over to a cabinet and pulled out a coffee can that had been there for years. He pried the lid off of it and dumped the contents out on the top of his oak desk. Several hundred human teeth clattered out in the warm light of the desk lamp.

"Problem solved," said Jimmy to himself. "Paleo dentistry at its finest."

Jimmy just had to start picking up bones where he found them. If they were missing teeth he would just plug a new one into the spot like a modern implant. This would require some practice on his part but not much. Jimmy figured he could do that with skeletons too. If he were missing some vertebrae, he would simply find the missing part and cobble an intact skeleton back together. Fibula, tibia, jaw, it didn't matter, Jimmy was seeing dollar signs again.

Just as he began his mental journey back in time when his phone rang and startled him back into reality.

Chapter 13

Jake and Doc had just had their second cup of coffee filled by the waitress at Rio's when Bobby arrived. Doc was talking to her, asking questions to a contrived story that he made up as he went along.

"My nephew came through here this morning. He was going duck hunting with my brother. They were going to eat breakfast here on their way up to the lake. Yeah, he's quite a kid. What time do you go to work?"

"I've been here since six. I don't recall seeing him come in today. It's been pretty quiet around here," she said.

"Jake, Doc, good morning again," said Bobby. He pushed Donny into the booth next to Doc.

"Okay, I figure they got about a four or five hour head start on us. I am pretty confident that they headed north because of the tire tracks I found at the road this morning," said Bobby.

"I guess it's a start," said Jake. "What if you're wrong?"

"I haven't thought about that but I feel pretty strongly like this is the direction their headed."

"Along with ten thousand other vehicles," said Jake.

"Perhaps, but I have an idea. It's the middle of cane season and the citrus harvest is in full swing too. Pan Caribbean has a hundred tractor trailer rigs on the road right now. Some of them are going as far north as Titusville, others east to Vero or west to Tampa. I can talk to all of them," said Bobby as he pulled one of the two way radios out of his coat pocket.

"What do you think you can do with that idea?" asked Doc.

"Well, for starters, we have a description of the truck, said Bobby.

"There are lots of brown Ford trucks running up and down this road every day," said Jake.

"It's better than nothing. We are just going have to take our chances, it's all we have."

The men finished their coffee and went outside. Bobby activated one of the common channels on the radio.

"Good morning everyone. This is Bobby Alvarez. "I need your help today. I am looking for a brown F-250 four wheel drive pickup with a camper on it. We are missing some stuff from the number six field station and this vehicle was seen in the area. If you see it, give me a shout, no need to do anything else," said Bobby.

The radios in over a hundred vehicles crackled to life over an area of nearly fifteen hundred square miles. People in and on tractor trailers, tractors, pickup trucks, four wheelers, and at least one train heard Bobby's request. It wasn't long before someone called back.

"Hey Bobby, I saw a truck like you described a couple of hours ago heading south. It was pulling a boat," said the voice over the radio.

"Thanks for the call but this vehicle was not pulling a boat. I am pretty sure he was heading north too. I forgot to mention that," said Bobby.

"Okay, well I'll be headed back south later today, If I pass him going north I will let you know."

Junior, Hole, and Adam were making progress. So much progress that Junior missed the turn for State Road 60 and had to turn around and back track several miles to the turn off. He stopped briefly to get Hole a fresh ice pack from the cooler in the back of the truck. He walked around to the passenger side of the truck and opened the door.

"Here you go buddy. Your head isn't swollen as bad anymore. You just keep this ice on it and you will feel a whole lot better tomorrow," he said as he handed him the bag of ice. Hole winced when he replaced the bag and tried to smile a little. Junior pretended not to notice the flesh from Hole's head that was stuck on the old ice pack. He looked at the gunshot wound and noticed that the area of paleness had grown to about the same circumference as a beer can. It was white and reminded Junior of what a cadaver looks like after the blood has left it. The edges of it were dark red like the edge of a piece of beef that had been left in the refrigerator for too long. Junior was glad that the wound didn't seem to hurt Hole as bad as it did earlier in the day in the hours just after the incident.

The group continued on their way now heading east. They made it across the first river and continued on until they turned north once again. There was surprisingly little traffic. The landscape had turned from one of cane fields on an otherwise featureless landscape to one of a boundless prairie of pine trees dotted with cypress ponds. Except for the occasional minivan full of people heading to Orlando, the only other traffic was a sod truck or some other truck hauling agricultural products to points unknown. Junior turned east again and headed for his destination on the St. Johns River just like the plan called for.

Clarence and Lottie Pacynski had fought the launch day traffic for several hours and were happy to finally break free of the gridlock and be back on the open road. At eighty seven years old, Clarence liked to boast to his friends back home in Michigan about having witnessed thirty seven launches from Cape Canaveral. This year was no different for the couple with the exception of the brand new thirty two foot camp trailer they towed behind their brand new one ton dual wheel extended cab truck. It was a beauty and Lottie loved nothing more than to take pictures at each of their stops and email them back to friends and family in Michigan in hopes of receiving dozens of emails back from people noting how jealous they were, how beautiful the campground was, or what a nice rig they had. Lottie was always careful to include the local temperature and she never sent photos of a cloudy or rainy day. Today they were heading for a warm gulf beach to spend the remaining three weeks of their annual visit to Florida before returning home just in time to have their taxes prepared.

They traveled west on 192 in insulated comfort and talked about the space shuttle launch they had witnessed a few hours before. Clarence had become quite an expert regarding rockets. It seemed to most people that he encountered that he was an expert on just about everything, so much so that most folks couldn't wait for him to leave after listening to him for more than fifteen minutes.

The sun was high in the sky as the couple and their shiny rig crossed the river. Traffic was light and Clarence clipped along at sixty five miles an hour. Right after crossing the bridge he encountered a lumbering tractor trailer full of oranges that had pulled out onto the highway a third of mile or so ahead of him. Clarence pulled in close to the back of the trailer and cursed under his breath about how this would never happen in Michigan and how truck drivers back home knew how to drive. He accelerated around the truck with no traffic in sight. He passed the cab of the semi and nodded to the driver. By that point they were both moving around sixty five again. Clarence continued to accelerate until he was just about clear of the semi. Just as he started his plan to move back into his travel lane an gust of wind caught the big travel trailer. It sent the Pacynski rig into a minor fishtail. Clarence and Lottie's bedroom caught the front left side of the semi truck. The back of the camper was opened like a can of Spam and clothes and insulation, and all sorts of other items flew into space. The impact was felt as a dull thud in the cab of the pickup truck and was only momentarily destabilizing. The driver of the semi hit the air brakes hard and fought to keep his rig stable and on his side of the road. Up ahead he could see cars slowing down in the east bound lane. He fought the truck to keep it in control as fifteen thousand of the nearly fifty thousand pounds of Indian River ranges spilled over the side and top of the trailer with the sudden change of inertia. The impact put a tremendous force on the trailer tongue of the camper. It was wretched loose from the truck that towed it and the Pacynski's home away from home went careening off into the canal along the right side of the road. Smoke poured from beneath all the tires of the semi and the trailer and finally it came to a stop. People in the other lane had long since stopped to watch the spectacle and many of them were already out of their cars and were taking pictures. Others were stuffing bags with 'free' oranges. No one bothered to ask any of the people involved in the collision if they were okay. One person out of the twenty or so that were milling around did manage to activate the 911 system although he didn't stay on the line long enough to speak to anyone.

Six vehicles away from the wreck, sitting in the east bound lane sat Junior, Hole and Adams, stuck in the ensuing traffic jam.

"Holy shit! Did you see that?" Junior exclaimed.

"Yeah I did," said Hole. Adam just sat wide eyed staring out of the windshield. Evidently the 911 call worked because within twenty five minutes there was a helicopter from the Brevard Sheriff's office, a highway patrol helicopter, and two news helicopters circling high overhead.

Hole peered up in the sky at the airborne force circling overhead. Junior just sat there and took it all in. In a short while a couple of deputies and a highway patrol car showed up to assess the scene. As soon as they had everyone accounted for and determined there were no dead bodies in the debris they had traffic moving again. One by one the cars, minivans, and rental cars started to move. Oranges popped beneath the tires and soon the roadway was slick with orange pulp and fresh squeezed juice. Clarence, Lottie, and the truck driver were standing in the front of the semi truck answering questions for a highway patrolman. Lottie was being checked out by a paramedic because she was hyperventilating. Not because of the wreck but because she didn't know what she was going to write home about now. Her little world was sinking in the canal next to the road and she started to cry. Just as Junior passed the scene, Pepe Martinez, the driver of the Pan-Caribbean truck looked over at him then took a double take. When his eyes met Junior's they locked on like radar. Junior got an uneasy feeling and he picked up his phone and started dialing Jimmy to no avail. The signal was just not there.

Once the wreck was cleared, Pepe called Bobby over the radio.

"Hey Bobby! This is Pepe. I found your truck."

"Pepe, tell me more, where are you?"

"I am just west of the bridge over the St. Johns River on 192. I got in a crash when a couple of gringos from Michigan cut me off with their travel trailer. They just got the road cleared when the truck went by."

"What else?"

"Looks like there were three people in the truck, one of them was small."

"Where were they headed?" asked

Bobby.

"The only place they can head is east. It looked like the blinker was on at the bridge, like they were going to stop at the fish camp."

"Okay. Thanks Pepe," said Bobby.

"Bobby, there is one more thing. One of the dudes in the truck is messed up. Looks like something out of horror movie and I just got a quick glance. His head is messed up."

"Thanks for the update."

Bobby, Jake and doc heard the transmission and ran for their vehicles. Donny was already seated when Bobby jumped in, started his truck, and floored it. Jake and Doc were right behind him as they headed north out of the parking lot at Rio's.

Junior pulled into the fish camp and tried to call Jimmy again. It was no use. He packed some more ice into a fresh bag and handed it to Hole. By this time the wound on his head was devoid of flesh and the surrounding tissue was starting to peel away. Junior cringed at the sight of Hole. He started up the truck, pulled back out on the highway and headed east.

"Where are we going now?" asked Hole.

"I'll keep driving until I can get a hold of Jimmy."

"Okay. My head is feeling pretty good now and the swelling is almost gone. I'm glad I can see better now," said Hole.

Adam looked at Hole and winced and turned his head away.

Chapter 14

When Jimmy picked up the phone call there was no one there and he hung up. When it happened again about ten minutes later he could hear some crackling and couple of syllables that sounded sort of like Junior but the static was just too bad. After a half an hour went by it rang again and he could hear Junior clearly on the other end.

"Hey boss, you told us to call you when we got to the river but we couldn't connect so we kept driving," said Junior.

"Where are you guys at?"

"Just outside Melbourne," said Junior.

"So, I am planning on getting some stuff together here at the house then I am going to drive out and meet you at the landing on the river," said Jimmy.

"Jimmy, we nearly got in a hell of a wreck with an orange truck."

"Is everything okay?" asked Jimmy.

"Yeah, we're fine, Hole looks like shit but we are all okay. The truck smacked some yankee and his travel trailer, oranges everywhere, and the camp trailer is in the canal. Nobody got hurt though, don't know how that happened but everybody walked away."

"How's the kid?" asked Jimmy.

"I reckon he's okay. He got kind of quiet the last couple of hours, just stares out the windshield mostly."

"He's probably bored or hungry. You ought to get him some grub when you can. Maybe he's scared," said Jimmy.

"Maybe you're right. I'll try and get him

some food as soon as I can."

"What do you say we meet at the landing a little before dark. I'm gonna' get the big boat ready, make sure everything is working then head that way. If I get there before you, I'll do a little fishing but I will be within eyesight of the ramp," said Jimmy.

"I don't know Jimmy," said Junior.

"What do you mean? You ain't backing out or going to go off and do something stupid now are you?"

"Jimmy, when we went past the crashed truck it had a Pan Caribbean sign on the driver's door," said Junior.

"So what's that supposed to mean?" asked Junior.

"Jimmy, when I drove past that truck I was moving real slow. The driver was a Mexican dude and he just stared at me the whole time. Then he got on the phone or a radio and he called someone. I turned into the fish camp just long enough to fix Hole another bag of ice and then I left. I couldn't get a cell phone signal to let you know we were there so I kept driving," said Junior.

"That's kind of weird about the driver."

"Yeah, you know we were all around Pan Caribbean land while we were out at that site. Maybe he recognized us. I just don't know but I got a gut feeling that something is up with him," said Junior.

"I think you worry too much. Just in case though I want you to keep heading east. There are a couple of little motels out there right before you get to the interstate. Pick one and throw down there for the night. I am going to come on out, I can stay on the boat. If you're not there tonight, I'll drive in until I can get you on the phone," said Jimmy.

"Okay, I'll try and call you later on to let you know where we are bunked down," said Junior.

Junior drove east. Up ahead he saw a couple of buildings and as he got closer he saw that one of them was a motel. He pulled in slowly to the Fat Bass Motel. It was a ramshackle old dingy hold over from the 1950's that had traded hands dozens of times. The latest version attempted to cater to the fisherman who came out to try their luck on the St. Johns for a few days at a time. The neon light had burned out years ago and that's just as well because the big smiling orange had nothing to do with fishing and to Junior seemed a little confusing anyway. Out front was a plywood sign that could be seen from both travel lanes. It was hand painted and the huge largemouth bass painted on it had his mouth open with what looked like a rubber worn hanging from its jaw. The gills were flared and painted blood red and stood out against everything else because that was the only thing that ever got repainted. The fish was huge and disproportionate and was made even more grotesque by the small skiff in the background with the fisherman standing up in the bow fighting the giant fish. The man in the skiff wore a hat with ear flaps on it and he had a pipe hanging out of his mouth.

Junior rapped on the door with the word 'office' painted on it, probably by the same person that made the sign with the fish. He was just about to turn away when the door opened. The old lady standing inside motioned for him to come in.

"I need a room for a night or two. Do you have any vacancies?" asked Junior.

"What's it looking like to you? The parking lot ain't exactly running over out there is it? She responded.

"How much for a room?" asked Junior as he tried to prepare himself for the next snappy comeback.

"How many ya got?"

"How many what? Dollars?" asked Junior.

"No, not dollars, how many people."

"Three, no two ," said Junior.

"That'll be twenty six dollars a night plus tax. Towels are just finishing up in the dryer. Turn the air conditioner off if you leave the room. There's a couple of tackle shops up the road if you keep headin' east. There's also a restaurant up there. Food ain't too great but there's lots of it and the coffee is good. They open at four thirty in the morning, then they close, reopen again at noon 'till two and again at six."

Junior gave her a hundred dollar bill and she handed him the key.

Junior walked back out to the truck and pulled it up to the room. H parked parallel to the sidewalk in front of the room so he could sneak Adam in without anyone seeing him. He looked at Adam.

"I don't want any funny business from

you. I am going to open the room and then I am coming back out to get you. You aren't going to say anything, you're not going to scream, kick, bite or try o run away because if you do, I'm going to tie you out back of this place for the night," said Junior. Hole's grip on Adams' thigh cinched a little tighter and Adam grimaced. He didn't say anything, he just stared out of the windshield.

Junior went into the room and flipped on the only light. He started the old air conditioner and was happy to find cool air gushing from the dusty vent. He left the door open and stepped back outside to the truck.

"Hole, gimme' your socks," said Junior.

Hole looked at him for a second and the without question peeled of his filthy socks and handed them to him.

"Look kid, I don't want a trouble. If you yell these are going into your mouth," warned Junior.

Adam nodded and gagged. Junior took him by the arm and slid him across the truck seat. Once Adam had his feet on the ground, Junior hurried him into the room and came back out.

"Hole, you're looking sort of rough. I want you to do the same thing. Slide across the seat and get in the room."

"You ain't planning on putting those socks in my mouth are you?" asked Hole.

"Not planning on it," said Junior. He didn't know if Hole's question was an attempt at humor or if Hole actually was worried.

Junior spent the next twenty minutes

145

shuttling stuff from the back of the truck into the room. The beer was one of the first things and in the space of fifteen minutes, Hole had downed four of them. He was sitting on the corner of the bed closest to the door drinking beer and watching old carton re-runs. He positioned himself so there was no way Adam could get around or over him. Adam sat in the solitary chair on the other side of the second bed in silence. He thought about ways he could escape and what he would do first if he got the chance.

"There's only two beds in here," said Adam.

"What's your point?" asked Hole.

"I ain't sleeping in a bed with either one of you freaks," said Adam.

Hole threw an empty beer can at him which Adam evaded by ducking.

"We're going to hang out here for a while until the sun starts to go down. Then I'll go into town and see if I can find something to eat."

Junior picked up his phone and called Jimmy. After a couple of rings Jimmy answered.

"Where are you guys? Is everything okay?"

"Everything is fine. We're at the Fat Bass Motel. We got a room and we are all sittin' in here now waiting. Where are you?" asked Junior.

"I'm getting a few things together. I should be leaving in an hour or so. I'll call you when I get to the river and get the boat in the water," said Jimmy.

"Okay, just let us know."

Jimmy Goodland was happy. He would pick up another anatomy book or two from the flea market or the local bookstore. He remembered seeing one that had colorful illustrations of the human skeleton. He knew that he had hit on something big now he just had to put his plan in action. He jotted down notes to himself as he recalled details of some of the sites he had looted years before. In particular he was interested in the sites with the most bones. He couldn't believe it when he thought about it. All he had to do was get enough of the right bones to rearticulate a complete skeleton and he was in the money. Of course he never ran into anyone who was interested in this sort of stuff especially someone who was so generous. Jimmy had all kinds of thoughts running through his head. What if he could develop his own clientele, then he wouldn't have to deal with the outsiders from New York that he didn't know anything about.

Jimmy bounced out of the side door of his house and walked out to the barn and rolled the big door aside. Inside sat a thirty foot pontoon boat that he had spent years customizing. It had a heavy canvas cabin, a toilet, fifty gallons of water and several boxes of canned food on board. He had a generator, four bunks, light fixtures, rod holders, and plenty of seats. The very best part about the custom rig was a drop down ramp on the bow. Behind the ramp sat an ATV that was firmly strapped in place. It served as an expeditionary vehicle for Jimmy's adventures. Jimmy put two full propane tanks on the boat and secured them with elastic straps. He had two batteries that were on perpetual charge so when he did launch the boat he never had to worry with dead batteries. He hoisted both of them onto the deck. He attached the wiring harness from the engine to one of the batteries and went up to the console and turned the ignition switch. To his delight the motor fired up. He stashed a duffle bag with some clothes in it and then walked around the rig checking tires, lights, and other items. Once he was satisfied he ran the trailer jack up a few inches then backed his truck up until he was in position. Once he had the trailer secured he pulled the boat out of the barn and headed for the river crossing where he had sent Jimmy. It wouldn't take him long to get there.

Chapter 15

Jake and Doc were the first to arrive at the boat ramp Pepe had told them about. They were followed shortly by Bobby and Donny. The four men got out of their vehicles and stretched and had a look around. They walked down to the water and out on one of the floating docks. They looked up and down the river for quite a distance and they didn't see anything except for an occasional alligator. The men returned to the trucks and Bobby opened the tailgate on his and he and Jake sat down. He reached in a cooler and took out four sandwiches that he bought earlier in the day. The men sat and ate quietly.

"What now?" Jake asked Bobby.

"I don't know. We could wait and see if anything turns up, like that brown pickup that Pepe saw turn in here," said Jake.

The two men facing the water saw a solitary vehicle with a huge pontoon boat pull in front of the ramp. The driver carefully squared the boat with the ramp and then he got out. He unfastened the straps situate in the back of the trailer then got back into the truck and slowly backed the boat down the ramp. Once it was almost all the way in the water he got out of the truck again and unclipped the strap on the winch that held the boat firmly against the winch stanchion. He took a rope from the bow halfway down the floating dock and tied it off then backed his boat into the water. The whole operation went very smoothly. The man secured both bow and stern then pulled the trailer out of the water and drove far to the back of the property and backed the long trailer in and parked his vehicle.

"What in the world?" asked Doc.

Jake and Bobby turned their heads to see the boat.

"Think he catches a lot of fish off of that four wheeler?" asked Bobby. The men just chuckled.

The man who had just launched the boat went into the little tackle store and purchased a few items. Donny walked across the parking area to find the restroom. When he came out he found himself face to face with the owner of the big pontoon. Donny looked at him carefully.

"That's quite a rig you got there buddy," said Donny.

"Thanks," said the man and he turned and walked out to his boat, started it and pointed it north.

Donny trotted back over to where the rest of the men were.

"That's him," said Donny.

"That's who?" asked Jake and Doc simultaneously.

"I don't mean it's him, I mean that I seen this dude before," said Donny.

"So what the hell is that supposed to mean?" asked Bobby.

"I mean I seen this dude once or twice hanging out where us traders gather at the flea market. Once in Ft. Lauderdale and then a month or two later in Ft. Myers."

The men looked at each other then they looked back at Donny.

"That's it; they were all going to meet out here. That has to be it," said Bobby. "But for what" he asked himself.

"Then where are they?" asked Jake.

"Well, they're not here but they may be close. Maybe they got spooked by something. We know they turned in here," said Bobby.

"Let's wait here for a while and see if the brown truck shows up with Adam," said Bobby.

"I guess we could camp here until something happens or somebody runs us off," said Doc.

"Okay, then we wait," said Bobby.

The sun was staring to set when Junior decided it was safe enough to venture into town to try and find something to eat and buy some gas. He asked Adam if he would like anything special to eat. Adam didn't answer him. Adam was tired and getting depressed. He wondered to himself if he would ever be found and if he would ever see his family and friends again. He didn't show it but he was growing more depressed by the hour. Adam watched Junior pull out of the parking lot through the gap in the dirty curtains. It made him sick to be in the room with Hole, a feeling that was only made worse because he was in there by himself now. Alone with Hole now, Adam was scared.

At the boat landing Doc began to pace around back and forth. He was nervous and hated to wait on anything. He paced and thought out loud. Finally he couldn't take any longer.

"I'm going to take the truck up the road and have a look around," Doc told the others.

"Then what? What if you find something, what are you going to do then?" asked Bobby.

"I'll take care of it," said Doc as he

backed the truck out and turned it around.

"Don't go get yourself in any trouble Doc. If you need us, call us on the phone and if that doesn't work the radio will," said Bobby tossing one of the walkie talkies to doc through his open truck window.

Jake tipped his hat and pulled out and headed east.

Adam was still looking out between the dirty curtains when he thought he saw Jake's truck go by.

"Hey!" he yelled. It startled Hole so bad that he almost fell off the bed. He picked up the dirty socks from earlier and threw them at the boy.

"What the hell is wrong with you boy? What are you yelling at?" asked Hole as he got up to look out of the window.

Adam smiled his first smile since this adventure all began the night before.

"Nothing you need to know anything about," said Adam.

Hole stood up and took a step toward him. Adam bolted for the bathroom to lock himself in but just before he got the door closed, Hole managed to jam his hand in the door frame. Adam slammed it in a mighty thrust and Hole let out a howl.

"Boy I'm gonna' take care of you for that," said Hole as he leaned into the door with all his considerable weight and forced it open. He grabbed Adam behind the neck and pulled him out of the little bathroom and sat him on the bed. His hand was already starting to turn colors.

"I don't want you to even think about

moving," said Hole. Adam just sat quietly and suppressed the inner grin that had come to him when he thought he saw Jake's truck. He knew that if Jake and Doc knew where he was they would come get him and rescue him from these awful men. He tried to imagine the looks on the faces of Junior and Hole when Jake and Doc found him. He imagined them just down the road, planning to come save him and it made him feel better. He never once considered that the truck was just like hundreds of others on the road. He held fast to the idea that help was near.

Doc turned the truck around after driving for over an hour. He drove back out to the river. He passed the Fat Bass Motel again, this time in the dark. Adam didn't see him this time. Junior was less than a mile behind him heading back to the motel.

When Junior got back he tapped on the door and Hole let him in. Junior noticed Hole's discolored hand right away.

"What in the world happened to you?" Hole just turned his head toward Adam and grunted.

"I thought I told y'all to behave while I was gone,"

"It was his fault," said Adam. "He attacked me because I yelled."

"It startled me," said Hole

Junior cleared off the little round table under the solitary light bulb and set out his spread. He had a bucket of fried chicken, some gizzards, a bag of fried potato wedges that were cold and a half dozen packets of various highly preserved pastries. He also had a twelve pack of beer and another pack of some kind of discount soft drinks.

"Y'all eat up. It won't stay fresh forever," he said.

Junior had been feasting since he left the truck stop where he purchased the food. He stepped back outside and called Jimmy.

"Hey Jimmy, we're here at the motel. Getting a bite to eat right now. How is everything with you?"

"I'm doing fine. Got the boat in the water with no problems, all systems go," said Jimmy.

"Jimmy, I been thinkin'. I don't know if we ought to try and meet up with you at the ramp. I mean there's people coming and going all day and night down there. Surely the law must make a stop there even if it is just a game warden."

"I been wondering about that myself and I got an idea," said Jimmy.

"What's that? I'd love to hear it because I don't feel too good hanging out here much longer," said Junior.

"I'm going to pull the boat out tonight. I'm going to come up to the motel. I want you to make sure that kid is quiet and still. If you have to put a piece of tape on his mouth, do it. You can tie him up if you want but if you don't have to, don't do it. When I get there, you, Hole and the kid are going to get in the boat and stow away. I'll drive back down to the river, launch it again and we'll be on our way. I need to fill you in on what we're looking for. I think you are going to be pretty happy," said Jimmy.

"Is it a treasure hunt?" asked Junior. I've

been meaning to ask but I forgot.

"It is a treasure hunt. It is a treasure hunt like you won't believe."

"That sounds real good boss. When will you be here?"

"When it's good and dark, 'gimme' two hours and I'll call you back right before I get there."

"We'll be waitin'," said Junior.

Jimmy cruised the boat downstream five or six miles and then turned it around and headed back to the boat ramp. He started the generator and flipped on a few of the many lights he had affixed all over the boat. It looked like a one man Christmas parade coming down the river in the otherwise back night. Once he could see the light of the traffic crossing the bridge he turned off all but the navigation lights and continued his slow pace. Every now and again he would flip on the million candle power spot light and make corrections in his course. When he arrived at the dock the black water was still except for the small disturbance the boat made during docking. When Jimmy moved about it sent ripples across the water. Jimmy walked across the parking lot to his truck and repeated the launch operation that he did earlier that day but this time in reverse. He got the big pontoon boat out of the water and turned right on the road and headed east.

Jake and Doc watched the man. Donny was asleep finally trying to rid his brain of the last effects of his drunken stupor from the night before.

"What do you think he is up to?" asked

Doc.

"I have no idea," said Jake.

"I say we give him some time and then we go see."

"That sounds like a pretty god plan," said Jake who was also getting tired and bored doing nothing but waiting.

Jimmy was on the road now and nearly halfway to the Fat Bass Motel when he called Junior.

"Junior, I want you and Hole to take the kid and meet me behind the building but first you need to do something with your truck. I'll be there in fifteen minutes," said Jimmy.

"Okay, I'll park it around the east side right next to the motel, we'll be waiting for you behind the motel," said Junior.

"That sounds perfect."

Jimmy Goodland turned into the parking lot of the motel and continued to the east end of it. He made sure he gave himself plenty of room as he turned left around it passing Junior's truck which was tucked in tightly next to the wall. There was an old over grown rock garden partially hiding the truck that was full of some sort of ornamental cactus plants that were nearly as big as trees. Jimmy checked his distance again and turned left once more and he was behind the building. He had covered nearly half the length of the building when he saw Junior, Hole and Adam walking through a little breezeway between rooms. Hole had Adam by the nape of the neck with his good hand.

Jimmy didn't say a word as he pulled alongside of them. Junior stepped up on one of the wheels and into the boat. Hole struggled briefly with Adam and then handed him up to Junior who continued the hold on his neck. After Adam was settled into a spot in the back of the boat, Hole clamored in. Junior whistled to Jimmy and the rig began to move. Out on the highway Jake and Doc passed the motel.

Jimmy reached the road and accelerated. His truck was a little sluggish with the big load on the back but he made highway speed quickly. Once back at the ramp he launched the boat again but in half as much time as he took previously. He motored out of the boat landing area and headed north, downstream once again. Once the boat was safely out of sight he turned on a couple of dim lights.

With Junior, Hole, and the kid all on board now and the boat in the water, Jimmy felt more at ease. Adam never said a word. He sat on a bench seat behind the console and just looked around. Hole looked like he had a headlight on but it was reflection of the light off the round spot of bare skull that made it look that way. The light glinted off of it which made the wound even more grotesque. Adam didn't like the way it looked but he couldn't imagine how it must feel either. He found himself wishing that he could cover it and help somehow but at the same time he wished Sport would have had a magnum instead of a short round. In that case this would never be happening to him. He was tired and scared and he wanted this to be over. He longed for his mother and Jake and just wanted to be back at the ranch with his friends and family. He wanted someone to wake him up and shake him from this nightmare.

The boat moved quietly along the dark water barely leaving a wake. Jimmy moved the boat slowly along not much faster than walking speed. The sounds of the road disappeared quickly. Not even the whine of the Pan Caribbean trucks reached them now. They were in another world now. It was a wild and dark world that the men were comfortable in. The night was still but a slight breeze had begun to stir from the south and it grew stronger as the time went by.

"Hey Junior, come up here and tell me what you saw out on the canal bank," said Jimmy.

"We didn't get to spend too much time before the incident but there is a ton of stuff out there. I mean pottery, graves, bones, tools. I would love to get back out there in the good daylight and really look around," said Junior.

"Bones? Really? Was someone out there before you?" asked Jimmy.

"Yep but a long time ago. When they cut that canal they took off a slice of a burial mound and it scattered some stuff all over the place. It ain't ever been dug. It's thick in there and it don't look like anything until you're standin' on top of it. It's a pretty good sized mound but it's low to the ground. Nobody would see you in there even in the middle of the day," said Junior. Junior in keeping with his mentality never questioned Jimmy about why they were chugging down the St. Johns River in the dark. He just figured Jimmy was on to something and he and Hole would be dropped off to exploit it.

"Hey Junior, is Hole going to be okay?"

"I don't know. It don't seem to be bothering him none," said Junior. Hole just looked back at them and grinned, the bare spot in the middle of his head had begun to take on a life of its own.

Chapter 16

Jimmy was behind the motel when Jake and Doc passed by.

"I reckon he just disappeared," said Doc

"He's not too far. I don't think he can go too awful far with that boat behind him. Let's turn around and head back. We can get Bobby and Donny and go to town and find a place to bunk down for the night," said Jake.

Doc drove on without saying anything then the only thing that came out his mouth was, "Okay."

The pair approached the Big Bass Motel. They were moving a pretty good clip when all of a sudden Jake yelled out in an almost panicked tone of voice.

"Stop, stop the damned truck and turn in," he yelled. "I saw something.

Doc stepped hard on the brakes and they were nearly past the motel before he could safely negotiate the last turn in to the motel.

"Okay, okay, back up, back up now," said Jake as he fiddled in the glove box for a flashlight.

Doc cleared the end of the motel in reverse and stopped the vehicle.

"What did you see?" asked Doc.

Jake shined the light toward the side of the building and they both looked at each other. Junior's truck sat there cold in the dark. They got out and approached is cautiously with the light off. Doc had his pistol on his belt and it was ready to go.

Jake was the first to reach the vehicle and he shined the light into the cab .They didn't see anything. There was nothing there but some food wrappers, some old receipts for gas and some other junk."

They walked together to the back and peered in through the dirty Plexiglas window on the camper top. Again, lots of junk, camping supplies mostly but there were some old map tubes back there too. The two men looked at everything in the back. Each item was inspected for any sign of Adam but there was nothing there to indicate he had been in the truck. Jake noticed that Doc had drawn out a long rolled up piece of paper from on the tubes. There were markings all over it and notes that were hand written.

"Jake, this is the ranch. Whoever belongs to this truck has Adam," said Doc.

Jake held a small flashlight in his teeth and he unrolled the map on the hood of the truck. He felt the blood rush from his head.

"This is it. This is the canal, the village site. This is where the boys camped and here is where Donny's trailer sits," said Jake while pointing to the locations on the map with his finger. "These guys have our boy."

An hour had passed by the time they had finished looking over everything in the truck. Doc went around to the door marked 'Office' and rang the bell. After a minute or two nothing happened so he began pounding on the door. The same old lady who checked Junior in appeared in the small window next to the door in an old musty looking pink robe.

"What is it? What do you want? There are plenty of rooms, tell me which one you want and you can come back in the morning and pay for it," she said.

"I don't want a room, I want to ask you about a room," said Doc.

"Which room?"

"The one that belongs to the brown pickup truck," said Doc.

"Just a couple of guys down here fishing. That's all I know," said the woman.

"What's his name?" asked Doc.

"Why do you want to know? Is something wrong?"

"I was supposed to meet a friend of mine down at the boat landing. We were going to go fishing but he never showed up. His name is John," said Doc.

"Nope, not your guy, this fella is named Junior, sorry. I hope your buddy is okay. Weird things happen sometimes to people out on that river," she said and she drew the little curtain over the window and disappeared.

Doc and Jake hurried out to the truck. They were in a hurry to get back to the landing so they could share the first tangible evidence they had that the two people that duped Donny and took Adam were close by somewhere.

Doc headed back to the west careful not to speed too much. The last thing he needed now was to get stopped out here by one of the local yokel deputies and have to take the next two hours standing on the side of the road in oncoming traffic explaining why they were in a hurry, where they lived, what they were doing in the area. Finally they would have to endure the drug search after the deputy with the dog was located forty miles away and grudgingly made

162

his way back to where they were.

"Better get a move on," said Jake.

"I know, I just want to be careful. At some point we will need to get law enforcement involved but not right now," said Doc. "I don't want to draw any extra attention right now."

They continued on cautiously until they got to the turn off at the boat landing. Doc pulled in and almost right beside Bobby's truck sat Jimmy's pickup with empty boat trailer. It was neatly backed into a tight spot for anyone to see. Jake and Doc looked at each other.

"What do you think the deal is?" asked Doc.

"I don't know. Donny has seen this guy before around a flea market. Donny sells fossils at the flea market. The brown truck was out on the canal back where Donny's camp is which happens to be very close to where Adam disappeared," said Jake. I just don't know.

Doc pulled in next to Bobby's truck and blew the horn. Bobby got out of the cab and rubbed his eyes and walked over.

"What did you find?" he asked.

"We're pretty sure this guy with the big pontoon knows something. We found where the guys have been staying. I think they have Adam," said Jake.

Donny staggered over after being awakened.

"What's up, did you find Adam?" he asked.

"No but we found out that Junior is here somewhere. We think he has something to do with the person that owns the pontoon boat but I am not sure," said Jake.

Bobby dragged up some twigs and branches and a couple of knots from a pine tree and lit them. The fire danced to life and soon the men could all see each other well in the flickering light. They set out a couple of camp stools and talked over what they knew.

"I think if we find the pontoon we will find Adam," said Bobby.

"I think you're right. We need to find the boat and I think we will find Adam," said Doc.

"I am worried that now they have come this far, they may just dump him up there on one of the islands or put him out on the river bank. What if they hurt him?" said Jake.

"I don't think their intention is to hurt him Jake. They have him because of a stupid decision that the big ugly dude made," said Bobby.

"Yep, I think your right. The big ugly dude Hole. He was pissed that he got shot in the head. He just reacted because that's all he knows how to do. I imagine that they are trying to figure out how to get Adam back to a halfway safe place then haul ass and call the cops," said Donny.

"Surely there is something more to it. You don't end up kidnapping little kids because of a bunch of fossilized sea shells," said Bobby.

The men talked on for an hour in the dim light of the little fire. Jake stood up.

"We gotta' go find that boat. Bobby, I want you to go back to the ranch. Take Donny, you can trade off driving if one of you gets sleepy. I want you to go by my house and pick up my airboat. It's in the big barn out by the windmill. It's sitting there with the other boats. Donny, if something happens to Bobby I want you to go and get the boat and bring it to me. You can't miss it; it has Tiger Tail painted on the rudders. Get back here as quick as you can and we'll go get Adam," said Doc.

"Jake, I know you love that boat, I know it can outrun just about anything but I also know that you can hear it coming from two miles away. What if I bring my jon boat back? It's quiet, holds three of four people and a bunch of gear," said Bobby.

"You're right," said Jake. "I didn't think of the noise. What are you going to tell the girls when you get back?"

"I don't expect to see them. I'll call them and give them some sort of an update when I get close to town," said Bobby.

With that said he and Donny climbed into the truck and left for Clewiston.

Bobby and Donny drove into the night. They chatted on and off, each trying to keep the other awake. Bobby fiddled with the radio for most of the trip. For him it was the only way to tune Donny out of his mind so he could think about other things like finding and getting Adam back. Donny told stories about life when he was a kid. He talked incessantly about people he knew and people his family knew. It was a barrage of name dropping gibberish that Bobby couldn't care less about. People like Donny were a dime a dozen in the glades. They all knew someone important as if that would change things in their miserable lives. Bobby knew many people just like Donny. They knew everybody, they all claimed association with people who were rich, and they were always a day late and dollar short of making a fortune. Bobby thought back about all the assholes he met in his life that could get him out of legal trouble or make him rich because they were friends with the sheriff or the judge or they had inside knowledge of some great deal about to overcome their town, or they were perpetually involved in some other sort of get rich quick scheme. As far as Bobby was concerned, Donny was just another local loud mouth whose interests would be best served by keeping his mouth shut, especially now.

"I'm taking you back to your camp," said Bobby.

"What for? I want to help. I've come this far, I want to help save that kid. Plus I got a score to settle with Junior for what he done to me the other night."

"I don't know what's going to happen up there on that river but I know that the more people that get involved the more complicated things get. You need to stay here in case something happens here."

The two men turned off on the long canal road. They stopped momentarily and switched drivers then continued to Donny's camp. When they finally arrived everything was dark. They could see where raccoons had been in the garbage can. The door was still ajar from the activities from the night before. The whole place reeked of vomit, liquor, old food and cigarettes. It was cool outside and Donny pulled a folding cot and a sleeping bag out of the trailer and put it under the front awning and went to sleep. Bobby lay down in the cab of his truck for a few hours of sleep before heading back.

The next morning, Bobby got up when the first rays of the morning sun hit him. He started his truck, backed away from the trailer and headed out without saying anything to Donny. Donny never woke up.

Bobby drove to Doc's parents' home. They were out of town for several weeks and as far as he knew they had no knowledge of what had happened to Adam. He opened the big doors on the barn behind the house and backed his truck in. There were three boats tucked neatly in the back left side of the barn. Two airboats and his jon boat. Doc, Jake and Bobby all left their boats in the barn because it was central to where they used them most. The Tiger Tail was parked in the middle. It looked just as fine as the day it was delivered. Jake kept immaculate care of it. It was waxed to perfection and the metal flake glittered in the low morning light as it streamed through the open door. Bobby thought about it for a while. He thought about how they could run down just about anything out there and they could do it on dry land if they had to. He also knew that no one could sneak up on anyone in this boat with its powerful engine. Bobby backed up to the jon boat and hooked it to the back of the truck. He took a few items off one of the shelves and put them in the boat. Once he had cleared the barn he closed it up. He then pumped some fresh gas into both the boat and his truck and headed for the highway. Once he was underway he called Jenny.

"Jenny…we're going after Adam," he said.

"My God, I've been calling everybody, no one answers, what the hell is going on?" she fired back.

"It's a long story that we haven't heard the end of yet. We got lucky last night and we're pretty sure we know about where he is. There is no reason to think that he is hurt or anything from what we can tell," said Bobby.

"Bobby Alvarez, you tell me where you are right now because I am going to be there when you find my son," said Jenny in a stern voice.

"I will let you know something but right now I just can't because we don't have all the answers," said Bobby. With that he ended the call. His phone rang fourteen more times and it upset him that he left things with Jenny the way he did. He knew though, in his heart that if she came out to where they were things would get more complicated than they already were.

Thirty minutes out from the boat ramp on the river Bobby tried to call Jake and Doc. The reception was poor and he couldn't get through. When he finally made it the men greeted each other. Jake and Doc were happy that he made it back with the boat and that he was alone. They didn't want to have to put up with Donny for another minute. Jake started gathering supplies for the back of the trucks and stowing them on the jon boat. Doc helped him and soon Bobby was backing down the ramp. The wind had picked up a little more and it seemed like it changed a little from coming out of the dead south. It seemed as though there was a little bit more coming from just slightly east of where it had been coming from.

Once the boat was in the water Bobby started it right up. Jake got in first then Doc . He gave a shove off and they were on their way. They decided to head downstream to the north because that's where they saw the man and the pontoon boat earlier. It was dark and they didn't want to use lights fearing they would alert someone of their presence. They didn't move much faster than the drifting current. Every now and then Bobby would turn off the motor to just drift and listen, hoping to hear something but they never did.

Hours ahead of Bobby the pontoon boat pulled into one of the dozens of feeder creeks that it has passed. It opened up into a natural basin surrounded by cypress trees at water level. The elevation changed quickly and so did the landscape. Just a few yards up the bank the giant Live Oak trees started. Long beards of Spanish Moss drifted in the quickening breeze and Jimmy could just barely see it in the feeble light. It was one of the few things that Jimmy found to be spooky in the woods at night. Maybe because it was so animated as it flapped in even the slightest breeze. Whatever it was, it made the hair on Jimmy's neck stand up, especially if he was alone. He hopped off the bow of the boat with the end of a rope and he tied it off to the first sturdy limb he could find.

"This is it boys. This is where we are spending the night. Maybe lots of nights," said

Jimmy.

Junior looked over the railing of the boat into the black water and the cypress knees and thought about everything else that surely lurked around this place at night and how pissed off the local wildlife must surely be with this giant aluminum can sitting on top of them.

"Where the hell are we anyway?" asked Junior.

"Junior, we are likely closer than we have ever been to never having to work again," said Jimmy.

Jimmy's eyes lit up even through the fatigue of the last thirty hours.

"Man, that's the best thing I have heard in a long time."

"We need to get some sleep now but in the morning I should know something pretty quick," said Jimmy.

The boat was spacious. Everybody on board had a folding cot and a sleeping bag. Adam was already asleep. Jimmy dropped a couple pieces of split shot into an empty beer can and gently tied it around Adam's ankle just in case he decided to make a break for it in the night. Someone would hear it and likely stop him before he got off the boat. Soon everyone was fast asleep. The breeze rocked the boat slightly and the ripples slapped at the pontoons rhythmically, guaranteeing everyone would be lulled into a peaceful slumber.

Things weren't quite so comfortable for the crew of the jon boat. When Bobby had finally had enough he turned the boat hard to the left and accelerated. He stuck the bow far up on the bank and killed the engine. They sat there for a minute or two before anyone said anything.

"This is as far as I go tonight," said Bobby.

"Okay, this is where we camp," said Jake who already had one foot on the bank and the other in the bow of the boat as he lifted a bag of gear out.

The three men had packed jungle hammocks thinking they were lightweight and easily stowed which they were. But, they were hammocks and there wasn't a tree around anywhere close to where Bobby beached the boat. After looking around for a long time the three men were able to find enough sticks to be able to pitch the hammocks on the ground like one man pup tents and that is exactly what they did. They went to bed with no fire, no lights and nothing to eat.

The next morning, Jimmy was up before the sun. He unhitched the ramp at the front of the boat and gently let it down on the bank. He straddled the big four wheeler and started it up and drove it off the boat. Junior, Hole and Adam all woke up briefly but then rolled over and went back to sleep. He could see them moving through the clear plastic windows of the canvas cabin.

Jimmy picked his way up the bank. He turned sharply this way and that to avoid obstacles. Every fifteen minutes or so of forward progress he would stop and push a button on the GPS mounted on the handle bar to fix a new location in case he got lost. He wasn't wild about technology but he would readily admit that GPS had saved his ass on more than one occasion. It also helped him evade capture and find alternate routes out of sticky situations. While he was out on the river before he picked the rest of his crew up at the motel he carefully plotted two dozen likely locations on a satellite image of the area. He always had his trusty laptop with him and it was configured to a satellite phone so he could access the internet from virtually anywhere, rain or shine. He put the coordinates into the GPS. It took him an hour to reach the first waypoint.

Jimmy got off the ATV and walked around in a large circle. Seeing nothing of interest he moved on. A late cold front was bearing down on the region and the wind picked up steadily throughout the morning. By late morning Jimmy found himself back alongside the river. He was on high ground now surrounded by an ancient hardwood hammock of Live Oak trees, Hickory, palms, and even a few tall straggly citrus trees trying to reach the sun through the nearly impenetrable canopy. He stopped the ATV again just inside the edge of the forest and walked in. The back side of the area faced a large marsh that was covered in saw grass. The only thing that interrupted the marsh as far as he could see were occasional clumps of willow trees swaying in the breeze. The area looked more akin to a prairie and was likely dry enough to traverse most of the time. Jimmy walked the edge of the hammock in narrowing circles. The side next to the river was a natural harbor much like where the pontoon was tied out. The bank was steeper and there were fewer cypress trees. Jimmy walked along the bank just above where the black mud gave way to sand. He noticed shells. Lots of shells. There were oyster shells and clam shells lying about, bleached white from years of exposure. Certainly they had been brought there. The bank had been cut away at one point to fashion and landing area for some type of boat but it had been a long time since anyone had been in there with anything bigger than a row boat.

He spent most of the day walking the area. He was careful to move slowly and take account of everything around him. Snakes would not yet be a problem because it was still fairly cool. If it warmed up though Jimmy thought to himself that he better look down and pay attention. On his sixth circular trip around the site there was a pair of squirrels skittering around above him. Jimmy heard them and though he knew what was causing the commotion he clamored up to the top of the site forgoing the last concentric trip around it.

The dead leaves on the ground were damp and slick and smelled moldy. There were dead moss covered branches that he had to step over or go through. When he reached the top in the damp darkness of the late afternoon he stopped dead in his tracks. Between him and where the hill dropped off again was an apex of sorts, the top of the hill. Looking closely at it he noticed that it had been cut cleanly in half by something to a depth of nearly ten feet. The trench was carefully laid out between the huge oak trees in a straight line. He approached it and scratched his head. He thought about how this could be. He thought to himself that it could have been done with men and shovels but it would have taken a lot of them. He was certain he had found the work site of the eccentric and presently missing archaeologist but nothing was adding up. He walked up to the gash in the hill and put his hands on the sides like he was testing an old rope bridge. He stepped forward into the even darker chasm and proceeded forward. Eventually he saw light of the other end. He noticed small side diggings in the walls of the trench and he felt things cracking beneath his boots like he was walking on light bulbs. He cleared the trench and turned to look where he had been. He had a weird feeling that he had just come through some sort of a time warp but Jimmy felt like that often when he was robbing a site. The hair stood up on his neck which was a feeling that was not to unusual for him. He was alone now and it was always more pronounced when he was alone. It was very quiet, even the squirrels had left.

Jimmy tuned back around and headed down the side of the hill through the trees when he saw it. He was no more than a hundred and fifty feet from where he emerged from the trench. The ground flattened out under and expansive moss draped oak with dozens of low slung limbs, some of them sweeping the ground. To the side was a miniature back hoe that must have been used to dig the trench. One of its tiny tracks was off of the idlers and stretched out behind it. It probably hadn't been moved in a year. There was a canvas tarp stretched between some of the limbs and pulled tight. It was covered with soggy leaves and had caved in on one corner and there was a wooden table under the tarp. Two rusty kerosene lanterns swung under the tarp in the breeze. There were four folding chairs situated around the table and in the most macabre scene Jimmy had ever witnessed, four complete skeletons were seated at the table. The bones were stained dark brown from hundreds of years of tannic acid leaching through their graves. They stared back at him with lifeless eye sockets. Jimmy noticed that the teeth were perfect. He approached the table quietly and just stared. Beyond this scene there was another large tarp stretched over a limb. There were three sides to this area and a cot in it. There were some old moldering free standing shelves with all sorts of stuff stacked on them. There were a few books growing some sort of black mildew, their pages hopelessly and forever glued together by the digestive process going on between them. Other shelves had ceramic pots lined up on them and other had different pieces of skeletal anatomy from jaw bones to long bones. Jimmy saw what he always called a 'wish bone' sitting there. He could never remember the correct term hyoid even though he studied his old anatomy books all the time. It didn't really matter what he called it, he just had to remember where it went. He was determined to not leave anything out once he started delivery of skeletons to his new friends in New York.

Jimmy dug through the items on the shelves as he gently brushed the spiders and ants away. He found a canvas bag which he opened up in the dim light and six gold coins shined back at him. He put them in his pocket and turned and walked out from beneath the shelter and sat down in a crook of one of the low limbs. He wiped his face off and thought for a little while. If he could get this material out of here without anyone seeing him he would be rich beyond anything he ever thought possible. He trusted Junior and if Junior trusted Hole then he was okay. No one knew they were there. He would deal with the kid as things came up but he surely didn't want to hurt him. He just wanted him to go away but Jimmy couldn't think of any good way to make that happen at the moment. Maybe later they would drop him off at a truck stop or restaurant and call the cops after they put some distance between them.

Jimmy probably had close to fifty thousand dollars in his pocket right now and there was still the prospect of the site down in the Glades. He was anxious to get more. He got up, walked across the hill and down the other side. When he reached the ATV the wind was blowing steady out of the east southeast and the clouds had thickened even more. In a little while it would be dark again. Before he got back to the boat it started to rain.

It was still barely light out when Jimmy arrived. He backed the ATV up the ramp and tied it down with the straps lying on the deck. He untied the boat and walked back up the ramp. He grabbed a pull rope attached to the aluminum ramp and pulled it back and secured it. To this point he hadn't said too much other than they were moving. He started the engine, backed out far enough to turn the boat around and headed out to the main channel of the river. Once underway he called Junior over to a small table where he unrolled another map. He oriented Junior to their location and pointed to a place just a short distance downstream to a spot they were moving to.

"What did you find out there?" asked Junior.

"You won't believe me if I tell you. You're just going to have to see for yourself." Jimmy reached into his pocket for the coins which he spread out in single file across the map.

"Hot damn. You're right my friend, I would not have believed you. What else?" asked Junior.

"You'll see," said Jimmy.

The pontoon traveled another mile to an obscure creek on the west bank of the river. The big boat barely fit through it at the narrow places. The creek finally opened up to the natural harbor Jimmy had encountered earlier in the day. He pulled the boat up to the same spot that had been previously used to offload gear and undoubtedly the mini track hoe that now sat broken down. He let the ramp down and tied the boat off. The rain had started falling steadily.

Jimmy got off the pontoon boat at the new landing and scurried up the embankment. He oriented himself and in no time found the mound with the trench cut through it. He trotted back down to the boat for the others. They gathered battery powered lights, some basic tools, shovels, picks, a saw and a few other things. Jimmy and Junior made the first trip with the load of gear. They returned soon for more, this time they would bring Hole and Adam.

"Hey boy," said Jimmy. He refused to call him by name. "I know you ain't like this but I have to put a blindfold on you because I don't want you to see where you been."

Adam just winced as Hole stood him up and walked him over to Jimmy. The bare spot on Hole's head seemed to shine even brighter the closer he got to Jimmy. Jimmy took a step back and Hole stopped.

"Hole, I want you to blindfold the kid," said Jimmy as he handed him a dry rotted bandanna from beneath the console of the boat.

"Sit down," said Hole and Adam turned and sat on an ice chest. Hole secured the blindfold the best he could and he forcibly stood the boy back up and turned him toward the bow of the boat and then walked him across the ramp onto dry land. Adam knew that his feet were finally on the ground again. Even this little gesture made him feel a little better than he had in hours. He knew he could run across dry ground which was a huge improvement over swimming in an alligator infested river in the dark.

The three men and the boy made their way around the mound to the canvas with the table where the skeletons were seated. Jimmy took one of the plastic tubs they had and took one of the skeletons apart. It had been wired together with thin copper wire that he could easily with the wire cutter from the tool box. He stacked the bones into the tub.

"Man this is too weird," said Junior. "Why would anyone do something like this? What do you want with a bunch of bones anyway?"

"I'll explain later," said Jimmy. "Put the boy in this chair and tie his hands behind him for now."

Hole plunked the boy in the chair and tied his hands the best he could. Adam felt the old dried rope and he noticed it wasn't much bigger than string. Hole was in awe of what he was witnessing all around him. He tied the boy to the chair while he looked around in the low light the others had cast from their headlights. Hole was not able to wear a headlight because of the wound on his head Jimmy managed to find a small light that could be clipped onto the bill of a cap. He gave it Hole who looked at him and smiled. Hole got up from his knees and walked over to the little track hoe and climbed into the operators seat. He fiddled with some switches and pulled on a button. He turned the key and it started up. Jimmy was astounded but the noise bothered him.

"Hey, turn that damned thing off. We can try tomorrow once we know we are alone for sure out here," yelled Jimmy through the noise of the little three cylinder diesel engine. The engine stopped and Hole hopped back off the seat and walked around the back of the little machine. He was determined that if digging was going to take place he was going to avoid all the shovel work he could. Hole examined the track lying on the ground. He picked it up and pulled it this way and that shaking the leaves and debris off of it. He broke some of the rust loose too and soon the entire piece was fairly flexible in his hands. He looked around and found two hand operated come-a-long winches that he fooled with for a while and soon he had them freed up and working.

Jimmy was steadily stacking the second skeleton on top of a piece of clear plastic that he had laid over the first one. He heard Junior yelling. He dropped everything and tool off down the back side of the hill.

When he found Junior he couldn't believe what he saw. There were two old cars sitting down on their frames. The tires had long since turned to cracked black dust. Oak leaves had accumulated around the cars to a depth of almost a foot and green slimy moss had grown all over them but was especially thick in the shady areas along the bottom third of the sides of the vehicles.

Junior just stood there looking into the driver's side window of a 1972 Coupe de Ville. Seated in the driver's seat as if going out for a Sunday drive was another skeleton. This one had a piece of cloth tied around its forehead. Tucked into this band and facing backwards was a large flight feather from a turkey. Seated next to the driver was a life sized effigy carved from the single trunk of a tree. It was the now famous Key Marco Cat. It was staring smugly out of the window with the same curious smile found on the only other specimen known.

"Jimmy, this thing is priceless. I mean it is beyond priceless. No one has ever seen one of these that is this big. The other one is tiny. You could put it on your shelf and use it for a bookend," said Junior.

Jimmy turned and walked back to where

their supplies were stashed. He tugged briefly on the rope that held Adam. He returned quickly to where Junior and the cars were with a crow bar and a large plastic tub. He put his hand in the door handle and his foot on the side of the car and gave it a yank. It came open surprisingly easy. So easy that he fell back in to the wet leaf mold. He picked himself back up and went to work disassembling the skeleton in the rain. He gave Junior a large piece of plastic sheeting and told him to take the statue out of the car and roll it up in the plastic.

When the men were finished, Jimmy walked to the back of the car. He carefully and expertly placed the working end of the crow bar beneath the lock on the Cadillac's trunk and easily popped it open. He shined his light into the trunk and there he found twenty four perfect ceramic pots lined up in three rows.

"We need to figure out how we're going to move these without breaking them," he said as he closed the trunk back down.

Jimmy's head was spinning. He hadn't even looked in the other car yet but the dollar signs were rolling through his mind like the wheels on the slot machines back at the reservation. The same slot machines that had parted him of so much of his hard earned cash. The analogy was precisely what allowed his conscience to let him rob graves. He figured he threw enough money away at Indian gaming casinos, why not just take some back. It was the self-perpetuating pattern of narcissistic thinking that put him at odds with everyone throughout his life and was one of the primary reasons he didn't have any close friends. Who needed friends when you had plenty of money anyway? Jimmy could always manage to buy what he needed and that included people.

They got back to where Adam and Hole were. Hole was out in the rain still tugging and pulling on the thrown track of the back hoe. Jimmy walked over and lit one of the lanterns hanging under the canvas. The little flame didn't overcome much of the darkness surrounding them. Jimmy loosened the bandana covering Adam's eyes.

"There's not too much to see here right now boy. Do you need a drink or something to eat?" asked Jimmy.

"I need to piss," hissed Adam. "I need to stand up." Just then Adam's eyes began to adjust to the light. He looked across the table and saw the three remaining skeletons sitting there like they were having Thanksgiving dinner together. He couldn't believe what he was looking at and after he thought about how he sat there with the bony table guests for over two hours he shuddered.

"Hole, get over here," called Jimmy. Hole got up and walked over to where they were. He was soaking wet but it didn't seem to bother him. He seemed to be immune to everything.

"Put a rope around his ankle and tie it good. He has to go to the bathroom."

Hole withdrew a length of chord from the waistband of his sodden pants and tied one end of it around Adam's ankle in multiple non-descript knots. Jimmy untied Adam's hands once he knew the rope around his ankle was secure.

Adam stood and stretched his legs and took a couple of steps toward the tree. He felt the tug of the line as Hole tightened it up. Hole doled out the line like someone would with a dog they didn't trust. Adam eventually made it out to the tree and relieved himself. He walked back over to his seat. Hole reeled him in like a fish and never let the line go slack. Adam sat down again and just stared shell shocked at the skeletons at the table.

"Want something to eat?" asked Jimmy who handed him a semi cold egg salad sandwich from the gas station. Adam took it and ate half of it. Jimmy gave him a bottle of water to help wash down the stale bread and tough eggs. After Adam swallowed it, Jimmy gave him a candy bar that went down a whole lot easier.

Jimmy and Junior returned to the cars with several more of the oversized plastic tubs. The second car didn't have a driver in it but the trunk was equally full of priceless pots all neatly aligned in rows. Hole went back to work on the track hoe. He tied the other end of Adam's line around his waist. He figured if Adam made a run for it all he would have to do is yank him off his feet and reel him up.

Jimmy and Junior returned once again. They sat the tubs down. In all they had four of them filled to the top with the items they collected from the cars. The cat effigy was lying on the ground next to the tubs. They rested for a while then each of them picked up a tub and started for the boat in the wind and the rain. After thirty minutes they returned only to pick up the remaining tubs and trudge back down to the boat. It was colder now and the wind was blowing hard. The rain came down harder and they all started to shiver except for Hole. On the last trip up, Jimmy pulled out a woolen army blanket and covered Adam up with it.

Hole found a grease gun among the items the archaeologist had stashed around his camp. It was lying in a wooden box along with several cans of sardines and some beef stew. He found eight cans of little sausages too. Hole pulled the lid off one of them and drank the thick juice from it. The sight of Hole drinking sausage juice from a can in the rain made Adam gag again. He had always hated those things because of the slime they were packed in. Hole turned the little can up and tapped on it and the little wieners slid out and into his mouth in a wad. He chewed once then swallowed the whole lot. He repeated this three more times to Adam's dismay. The labels on the cans had long faded away. Next, Hole popped open a can of sardines packed in mustard sauce only this time he chewed the contents for a long time. Once he swallowed the little fish he turned up the can and drank the greasy yellow sauce down. Some of it missed and ran from the corner of his mouth. It dripped down in fat drops of yellow and fell on his shirt. Adam might has well been looking at Frankenstein. When Hole was finished with his meal he wiped his mouth with a long satisfying pull of his mouth across his shirt sleeve and he went back out to the machine to resume his work.

Jimmy and Junior returned once more for the effigy. It was late and they were tired and cold. The two men tried several different ways to carry it but they finally settled on trussing it under a long pole. They positioned themselves, one on each end. Jimmy gave a three count and they stood simultaneously. They walked slowly off. When they cleared the back side of the mound, Hole got back in the operators seat of the machine and started it back up. Jimmy and Junior could hear it. The rain had stopped now and the air was very cool. The sound travelled very well and it seemed to get even louder once they were at the boat because it traveled very well across the water.

Hole jockeyed the track hoe back and forth until he was satisfied with its position and he shut it down again. He hopped off and used the cable winches to manipulate the track. He looped one end around a large Live Oak limb and the other end he fastened to the track. He ratcheted tension on the cable and the two ends of the track came closer together.

Jimmy and junior trudged back into the camp for the last time of the evening.

"Hole, I thought I told you to keep it quiet until tomorrow," said Jimmy.

"I almost got it done," said Hole. Jimmy couldn't help but stare at the gleaming white circle of skull that dominated Hole's head.

"Okay, just try and keep the noise down," said Jimmy. Jimmy had the sleeping bags from the boat with him and he rolled one out for Adam. He rolled his out and left the other two for Junior and Hole who was still working on the track hoe. "We got a big day ahead of us tomorrow. We're gonna' dig some and if we find anything we'll need to go ahead and put it on the boat. This place is rich. We may need to make a trip back to the truck to offload. If that's the case we will need to spend some time planning," Jimmy told Junior. Jimmy mulled it over in his mind what he would do with the cache of treasure. He realized instantly that the only reasonable place to hide it would be at his house along with the other treasures he had accumulated over the years.

Jimmy and Junior continued to talk into the night. Jimmy never let on anything about the two moneyed buyers from New York. Why should he. They didn't know that he was already at the site. They didn't fully expect him to move on the site for another six months or so. Jimmy was making big plans and he made sure he would be the center of those plans. The guys in New York would have to wait. Then, when Jimmy was ready he would begin supplying them a little bit at a time. They would never know where the good stuff went. He would busy himself putting together perfect skeletons for years. He had enough pots already to last for a decade of horse trading with the yankees he struck the deal with. Life was good.

It was three forty five in the morning when they were all startled awake by a tumultuous noise that sounded like the discharge from a rifle. Jimmy was the first on his feet. He struggled for a second or two to get his light on. He looked around and saw Hole standing there with a twenty pound sledge hammer. Hole had taken a mighty swing at a pin on the track and he missed. The hammer struck the side of the machine with a huge report that he didn't expect.

Cold metal struck cold metal and the sound resonated in everyone's ears. Adam looked out over the edge of his sleeping bad. Junior was hopping around trying to get his leg in his pants. Hole took one more swing and the pin that held the track together was hammered home. He was done. He had a way to dig once the sun came up.

"What in the hell are you doing? Are you out of your mind? Did you hear that? Jimmy yelled at Hole.

"Sorry boss. I just wanted to get this thing working before morning," said Hole. He was an awful mess. He was wet and muddy. He had grease all over his hands and clothes. The mustard sauce from the sardines had dried to and unsavory brown crust. He smelled bad too but that was nothing out of the ordinary for him.

"Why don't you try and get some sleep?" asked Jimmy. Hole put the hammer down and walked over to where the men were. He unrolled his sleeping bag and lay down on top of it and went to sleep.

Chapter 17

Doc, Jake and Bobby had been engaged in a miserable day of slowly moving down stream. They had been up innumerable creeks, ditches, interceptors, canals, and virtually anything else that led into the river that had water in it. Everything either ended in an overgrowth of cat tails and weeds or some sort of pump station or water control structure. They had enough fuel on board to make it all the way to Jacksonville if they had to but none of them wanted to. They made their way along in the dark and in the rain for over an hour when they came to another channel leading off from the main river. Bobby turned the boat into it and kept moving. They arrived in the same spot Jimmy had parked the night before. Bobby saw the dual keel ruts the pontoons left in the mud and the footprints and ATV tracks as well.

"They were here at some point," said Bobby. He shined a light around on the bank to the other could see.

"How long they been gone or where they went is anybody's guess. It's probably safe to say that he kept heading north. We're getting closer Jake. This isn't going to last forever," said Bobby.

Jake looked down momentarily and Bobby thought to himself that he couldn't recall ever seeing Jake like this.

"I can't get if it out of my head what must be going through that boy's mind right now. I can't close my eyes without thinkin' about what Jenny is feeling right now. I haven't talked to her in two days," he said.

"Jake, we're gonna' get the boy back. I don't know how you feel but I can imagine what you must be going through." said Bobby. He put his hand on Jake's shoulder.

"It's okay Uncle Bobby. I'll be alright. I know that Adam will be alright too. I am glad you and Doc are here."

The three got out of the boat and made camp in the rain. This time they were all able to eat a little. Bobby made some coffee over a small gas stove and the three of them sat and talked for over an hour. This time they were able to string their hammocks from tree branches which made them much more useful and comfortable.

Around two thirty in the morning the rain stopped and the wind got a little stronger. At three thirty there came a loud crack like a rifle shot in the distance. It stirred Doc but Jake was fully awake having slept just fitfully on and off since their arrival.

"Jake…are you awake?" asked Doc.

"Yeah. I'm awake. I heard it too. It didn't really sound like a gun but it was loud enough to be a gun," said Jake.

"I think we need to head that way. Whatever it was is close enough. As long as there is nothing in between us and where that sound came from we should be on top of it in a half hour," said Bobby who was now wide awake as well.

The men dug around in their bags for a few items. They each took a bottle of water, a knife and a length of rope. Bobby had his .45, Jake had his .30.30 in a scabbard on his back. Doc had his old shotgun on a strap around his shoulder. Bobby took his phone and one of the company radios.

Bobby checked a compass against one of the maps Jake and doc brought back from the motel.

"I don't know what we'll find out there but if we see or hear Adam, we get him first. If we don't have to tangle with these assholes then we need to avoid them. We have the dark on our side, let's use it to get as close as we can," said Bobby.

The three of them set out and clamored up the bank. They picked their way through thick underbrush and vines as they pushed north at a very slow pace. They followed a natural trail along the river for a long time. The air was cold. The stiff breeze helped mask the occasional twig breaking underfoot but it also masked everything else including voices like Adam calling out.

They walked, climbed and pulled their way along in the dark. They stopped every ten minutes to listen then they moved forward again.

All three of them were exhausted by the trudge through the woods and the events of the last forty eight hours. They were four hundred yards from Adam and didn't know it when they sat down to rest. It was a quarter to five and they all sat down. All of them dozed off.

The very first rays of sunlight couldn't get through the canopy of the dense hammock but sound traveled easy in the crisp air. Not far in the distance the three men woke up to the sound of a small diesel engine an soon afterwards the rhythmic clack of a tracked vehicle on the move. Jake sprang to his feet in a dead run with Doc right behind him. Bobby grunted to his feet and took off after them. In a loud whisper he asked them not to do anything stupid.

The sound of the machine grew steadily louder the closer they got. Soon Jake and Doc were at the bottom of the hill. Bobby joined them after a few minutes. He was huffing and puffing while he tried to catch his breath. The three of them collected their breaths and sat squatted across each other. Bobby was the first to speak.

"I think you two should crawl up there and see if you can get a better look. It's still dark and you're not going to get a better chance. I'll go around this thing and try and get on the back side of it in case you need me over there. I don't know what's up there, it may me nothing but a farmer or something," said Bobby.

"Okay," said Jake. He stood up and walked a few steps up the side of the hill. Doc walked down the way another fifty feet or so and looked over at Jake then the two of them started their short ascent. They met back at the top, both of them lying on their bellies.

"Jake," whispered Doc.

"What?"

"Do you think bobby has enough sense to get out of the way if we start shooting?" said Doc and he started chuckling.

"I hope we don't have to shoot," said Jake.

The two of them peered over the top of the hill. They couldn't see much in the dark but what they did see astounded them. There was the outline of people sleeping under the canvas tarp. One of them was much smaller than the other two. To the right of them the little track hoe was making its way up the hill on the far side of the trench. They could make out the outline of a big man driving it but in the low light the details were lost for now.

Bobby followed a similar course on the other side. He emerged closest to the machine creeping up the hill like some sort of prehistoric insect. He couldn't really get a good look either but he could see through the dim light and undergrowth that the machine was yellow. He sunk back down out of sight and waited.

Jake and Doc continued their vigil and after a while one of the men in the camp began to stir. He got up and fired a small camp stove and put a pot of coffee on it. Jake and Doc were so close that they could smell the coffee and the aroma spread out under the light fog and down the edges of the hill. Both of them longed for a cup of it but quickly dismissed the idea when the second man rose up out of his sleeping bag. The two of them filled their cups and walked out from beneath the tarp over to the mound with the gash in it. They talked for a while and returned to the camp under the tarp.

Finally, the only sleeping bag left began to move and out popped Adam. Jake nearly convulsed when he saw him and Doc had to put a hand on him to keep him from charging through the camp to rescue the boy. Jake pulled out a small pair of binoculars and wiped the lenses with the tail of his shirt to try and get rid of some of the condensation on them. He put them up to his eyes and glassed the area. He swallowed hard and turned to Doc.

"Jake, you need to listen to me. You gotta' promise me you are going to stay put. I want you to hear me out, we are going to have to make a plan," said Doc.

Jake just stared at him. "What is it? What did you see? Tell me what you saw," said Jake.

"Jake, Adam is there. He looks okay but he is sitting at a table with skeletons."

"What do you mean a skeleton? A skinny man?"

"No, I mean skeletons. These guys are up here robbing graves. There are skeletons sitting at the table with Adam," said Doc.

"Let's go now," said Jake. "I can shoot the one under the tarp, then the one on the tractor, when the third one runs out from that trench, you can shoot him. We'll get Adam and leave. By the time they find these guys no one will ever know what happened."

"Jake, you need to listen to me. There are three of them. We don't know if they are armed. We don't need any bullets flying around here with Adam in the middle of it all."

Doc could see that Jake was thinking about everything from running in and killing everybody to sitting by and waiting until they got some kind of a break. The two men sat and waited. The watched Adam move about and they saw that he was offered food and drink and he had the opportunity to relieve himself as well. When Adam got up and walked Jake noticed that he had a cord tied around his ankle, the other end now tied to Jimmy. Jake was furious but he held on. They were trying to get a feel for what was going on. They tried to see how the men came and went and if they ever did anything the same way twice.

The other man gathered up a few items including a trowel and a small box that had a wired bottom in it that presumably he used for sifting. He made his way over to the trench and walked into it. After about thirty minutes he emerged from the other side. Doc and Jake couldn't see where he came out from where they were. Soon the man was standing on top of the hill and was standing next to the man who operated the track hoe. The two of them talked for a while.

Doc looked them through the binoculars," Holy smoke," he whispered under his breath.

"What is it Doc," asked Jake.

Doc handed Jake the glasses.

"Oh my God. That has got to be the most horrible excuse of a human I have ever seen. Look at his head. What the hell is the deal with his head?" said Jake.

"That's the dude," whispered Doc. "That has to be the freak that Sport shot in between the eyes. That's Bobby's medicine man."

"You're right. I wonder what happened to his head beside the .22 short hitting it."

"I don't know but it has to be killing him," said Doc.

Jake continued to watch Hole through the glasses. He could see tiny gnats forming a cloud around the wound and every now and then a large shiny blow fly would land on the edges of the bare spot for a quick snack before getting waved off.

The two men talked for a while then they both walked down off the top of the mound toward the base of it where the big trench started. They entered the trench together and after about twenty minutes they emerged together. Junior had a sack slung over his shoulder that was dripping muddy water. Junior and Hole trudged back up to the top and continued to talk.

Across from Jake and Doc, Bobby had managed to slither himself around and down to the opposite end of the trench. He could almost see through it. With the exception of one slight bend in it he could have. He saw Hole and Junior leave the top but he didn't have any idea about what happened next.

Jake turned his glasses on Adam again who seemed to be calm for the moment. Jimmy busied himself around the camp stuffing different items into bags and tubs. He scurried about like a rat in a maze stuffing items in his pockets as well. Junior walked down from the top of the hill and the two of them struck up a conversation.

"I walked into that cut," said Junior.

"What did you find in there my friend?" asked Jimmy.

"Lots of material. The guy was a perfectionist and I don't know how he did it. Maybe with some of the newfangled ground penetrating radar they got now," said Junior.

"What do you mean?"

"Well, if you walk through there, and I only went about halfway, he cut right up to the edges of four graves. That's all on this side mind you. I mean it is like walking into one of those three dimensional museum displays. All along the bottom of the thing there are pottery shards scattered and a bunch of clam shells and other kind of shells." said Junior.

"Can we get the stuff out?" asked Jimmy.

"We can but we are going to have to dig it out. That's why the guy had the little back hoe. The soil is like concrete, some kind of marl with bits of ground up shell in it. Packs real hard. Down at the bottom though it gets kind of soupy because of the rain," said Junior.

"So what do you suggest?"

"I talked to Hole about it and we come up with the idea that one of us would be in the trench and the other would work the back hoe. One of us could identify places that need the extra power of the back hoe. After the back hoe, a man could finish carefully with a shovel or a trowel.

"When do you want to start? You know we're going to have to work fast and get the hell out of here pretty quick," said Jimmy

"I figure in another hour the sun will be high enough to shine some more light into the trench so we don't have to work by headlight or feel," said Junior.

Adam listened intently at their conversation. He pretty well knew what they were all up to. He always tried to figure out where they all were even though he couldn't always determine it. That had changed now because they forgot to put his blindfold back on him this morning. Not that it really mattered because he really didn't know where he was. He knew that he had been on a pretty long car ride, then a boat ride, then another boat ride, and now he was here sitting with skeletons watching people steal stuff from other skeletons. He struggled with idea for a long time because so little of it made sense. Now that daylight came he struggled more about what he had to do to get away. He planned in his head which way he would go and what he would take with him.

Junior returned to the top of the site. He talked with Hole a little longer and the two returned to the base of the excavation. Hole went in and went to work. This was his forte and he couldn't wait. It didn't matter what he was digging for, he just loved to dig. He dug all his life. It didn't matter if it was a pipe under a road, and new sewage system, old system, electrical system, he just loved it. He was the consummate ditch digger and he had been doing it since he quit the eighth grade at the age of fifteen. Treasure hunting was just another thing to dig for him.

"Now Hole, I want you to be careful. This is a little different than the other times we worked together. This time I don't want you tearing through bones and throwing them everywhere. If you find some I want you to come up and get me. We can take them out gently and in order and we'll put them in a box," said Junior.

"How come we gonna' do that? It's just gonna' slow us down," asked Hole.

"I don't ask questions. That's what I been told, that's what we're gonna' do. This is the biggest thing we've ever done. I still ain't sure of exactly how big but Junior told me that if we do everything just right and we don't get caught, and no one gets hurt, we'll never have to work again," said Junior.

Hole looked at him and just grinned. The gnats swarming around his head were increasing in numbers as the morning sun warmed the air. There were three blowflies now ducking in at intervals to sample the spongy red meat and the yellow juice that was starting to ooze along the edges of the round wound on his head. Accustomed to insects and all sorts of other denizens during work, Hole simply brushed them away. He had a large beefy stain across the top of his right forearm from constantly swiping it over the spot on his head. Still, if it caused him pain he never let on. Junior went back over to the tarp and fumbled around until he found an old bandana. He found the red one that had been tied around the head of one of the skeletons. It was old and dirty and had darkened considerably from the mold and the weather. He brought it back out and helped Hole tie it around his head. He didn't want Hole to be distracted by his insect entourage but more importantly, he didn't want to look at the glaring piece of white skull anymore.

Jake nudged Doc to take a look. They saw Hole pick up some tools and head into the trench. Junior walked back to the top of the site and took a seat on the little machine. Hole reemerged after twenty minutes and he had his hands full. He brought out two pots and a couple of shell tools and laid them down in the sun. Junior trotted down to look and just smiled at him. Hole went back in and Junior went back up.

Another twenty or thirty minutes passed and Hole came out again and motioned for Junior to come down. This time they both went into the trench. They slogged through the soupy mud in the bottom of the dig. The rain from the previous day and night had finally percolated through the mound. When they reached the place Hole wanted to show Junior they stopped. Hole reached above his head to show Jimmy what looked like a tibia embedded in the wall. Hole took out a screwdriver and pecked at the soil around it. It was hard even though it was damp. Junior thought to himself that it looked like pictures he had seen of concretions but this material wasn't petrified. It was simply very fine particles of shell and white sand that had packed together over the last eight hundred to a thousand years. It was like soft rock but it wasn't rock.

"I can reach this with the bucket with no problem," said Junior. "I'm gonna' need you to come up and let me know the progress I am making since I can't really see down there. When I get close enough, you will need to let me know to stop."

"Okay. This is about where I want you to dig to. The rest of it I will get to by hand," said Hole.

Junior went back up and started the machine and swung the digging are out of the trench and lowered the bucket down. He could operate it but he wasn't good at it by any stretch. He hit the side of it pretty hard and the whole machine shuddered. It sent a cascade of debris down on top of Hole. Hole emerged from the trench mad and covered with dirt.

199

"Hey! What the hell you doin' up there anyway?" he yelled.

"Sorry about that man. I just need to get used to the controls. They're a little more sensitive than I expected. I'll try to more carful next time," said Junior.

Hole grumbled something to himself under his breath. His took a long swig of water and went back into the trench. Up above, Junior had taken another couple of swipes with the bucket. He was more careful this time and he was able to remove nearly a full scoop each time. The trench was situated north to south. Junior and the little machine sat on the east side and each time a scoop of material came up it was deposited on the west side of the trench. Presumably the spoil was to be pushed back in the dig after everything was done. Jimmy had set up a large shaker box that he found in the camp over on the west side of the trench. All he had to do was bring one of the fresh batteries from the boat and hook it up to the motor which was in turn hooked to an offset cam that shook the hell out of anything that went into the tray. He busied himself picking through the contents of the trays. Jimmy had long since taken the cord that held Adam to Hole and tied it to himself. The whole operation seemed to work in unison. Junior would dig, Hole would come up and instruct him and Jimmy would sift. Every now and then Jimmy would toss something into a coffee can next to the shaker so he could inspect it later.

Another two hours passed without anything happening. Doc and Jake seemed to be at a loss over what to do. The overwhelming impulse still was to go charging in with guns blazing, rescue Adam then leave. It was a great plan but left a lot of logistical questions that they couldn't solve. Namely, in the highly probable event that someone got shot, what would they do? They would have to rescue that person which meant hospital, paramedics, cops, and lots of people with lots of question. This was precisely what they wanted to avoid. If someone got killed then the potential problems would just be magnified. Again, something they didn't want to do. They also didn't know for sure where Bobby was. This of course left several unsavory possibilities that they didn't have an answer for.

"I'm gonna' go find Bobby and find out what the hell he is doing," said Doc. "I'll be back in a few."

"Okay, just don't let anybody see you," said Jake.

Doc slithered back down the side of the hill feet first and on his belly. He didn't have anything to worry about once he got to the bottom as far as anyone seeing him. He ran to the other side of the hill and saw where Bobby had started his long crawl up. Doc followed the same route. Once he approached the top he slowed down and crept up the rest of the way. He could see everything that he did from the other side. The only exception was that Junior was now facing him and he couldn't see Adam either. He looked around and saw signs of where Bobby had skittered off to the left and he followed them. He approached Bobby from below and slightly behind him.

"Bobby," he whispered. Bobby was so

startled that he nearly pissed his pants. "What the hell are you trying to do boy?" hissed Bobby.

"I came over here to see where you were. I figure if shit hits the fan, you don't need an extra hole in your head," said Doc.

"I see, thanks for the warm thoughts. I been right here watching this operation and I'm going to stay here. I think the machine operator is like the boss of the whole thing. If I need to I can take him out from right here with no trouble," said Jake.

"You do have a pretty good approach here. How will we know what to do though?" asked Doc.

"If I get into to trouble, I'll shoot three quick shots. If you hear that, come runnin'. If you hear one shot, just know that I got tired of sitting out here and I clocked the bastard in the head. Anything else, I'll just whistle real loud and then get a move on toward you and Jake," said Bobby

"Okay," said Doc and he turned and left. He thought that none of it really made any sense but at least he knows where Bobby is and Bobby knows about where he and Jake would be.

Doc got back to his place next to Jake. Things seemed to be just like they were when he left to find Bobby.

"Well, did you find him asleep over on the other side?" asked Jake.

"Nope, he's wide awake right in front of that digging machine, maybe forty yards or so. He's been watchin' everything since he got over there," said Doc. Before Doc left Bobby he looked all around for a landmark that would help orient him to bobby's location. Straight up over Bobby's head about thirty feet in the tree he was under there was a large pineapple shaped air plant about the size of a wash tub. It had a bright red flower spike coming out of it. Doc pointed in the direction of the air plant.

"See that plant in the tree," he said with an extended finger.

"Yep," said Jake.

"He's right under that with his pistol cocked. He said he may go ahead and shoot the guy on the hoe if something didn't happen soon. I told him that we just wanted to know where he was in case we did have to shoot."

"Doc, something happened while you were gone. That dude with the hole in his head was inside the trench working. He was coming out every time the back hoe took out two or three scoops. They would talk and he would make hand gestures and then go back. The dude's been digging for a while now, ever since you left. The man in the trench hasn't been back out. Just a minute or two before you got here a big gush of mud and crap came out of the end of the trench," said Jake looking at the man on the track hoe who was steadily working.

They watched the operation for another ten minutes or so and then the man hopped of the machine and went down to the entrance of the trench and went in. Junior was surprised to see the sides in the bottom washed out and undercut by a huge gush of water and mud that he failed to notice. Hole was nowhere in sight. He looked all around until finally he saw just the fingertips of a left hand sticking out of the mud. The trench had caved in and tons of water and mud like wet cement overwhelmed Hole and covered him over. He didn't stand a chance because once the fine mud covered him it quickly filled in all the spaces. Even the act of breathing caused the mud to pack even tighter around Hole's chest until he stopped breathing all together.

Junior ran out of the trench through the wet mud and grabbed a shovel and yelled for Jimmy. At first Jimmy didn't respond so Junior ran back out and up the west side and yelled to Jimmy for help. The shaker was a loud and obnoxious device that was impossible to talk over.

"What? What did you say?" asked Jimmy. Junior reached over and pulled one of the clips from the battery.

"The trench caved in on top of Hole. I think he is dead," said Junior.

"Aw shit," said Jimmy. "What are we going to do now? What do we do with a dead body?"

"I don't know but maybe he ain't dead. I need your help. Get over and get on that machine," said Junior as he took his shovel and ran back down the hill and into the trench.

Jimmy was close behind him. He quickly got into the operators seat and swung the bucket over the trench. Junior was already trying to dig Hole out. On Jimmy's third scoop the sides let go again and Junior Davis was inundated and buried right next to Hole.

Jimmy worked another ten minutes before he decided that he would get down and check out what had happened. Jimmy got off the seat and put his feet on the ground. When he turned to walk down the hill he came face to face with Jake Alvarez and his Winchester. Behind Jake, down at the table Doc had freed Adam and was exiting the area toward the old cars.

Jimmy ran around in front of the digging machine and stopped underneath the bucket that he had just withdrawn from the trench. It was dripping mud and debris all over his head when Bobby emerged from in front of him. Jimmy pulled a pistol from his waistband and leveled it at Bobby. Bobby already has his 1911 ready to go and he fired three shots none of which hit Jimmy. Jake had long since hit the ground when he saw the first pistol drawn and was content to stay there. Even though all of Bobby's shots missed their intended mark, two of them tore through delicate hydraulic lines that sent the tiny but full bucket along with its mechanical arm crashing down. The bucket hit Jimmy in the head in a glancing blow. Had it not been slick with water and mud it probably would have driven him down in the ground by several inches just like a tent stake. Instead, it hit the top of his head about two thirds of the way back from his forehead. The blow sent him sprawling on the ground face first. Jake tore around the machine and seized Jimmy, flipping him over on his back with one arm. He then pounced on him and sat astride the man with one hand on his throat and the other clenched in a fist up in the air over his head. Right as prepared to deliver his first blow he noticed that Jimmy felt flaccid underneath him. He was mush and nothing moved. Jake got off of him and looked at him. He was breathing and moving his eyes but that was all. The blow from the bucket smashed his third and fourth vertebrae. Jimmy would be in that position for as long as he lived. He would never feel anything below his neck again. Jake wanted to hurt him. He wanted to kill him with his bare hands for what he had taken from him and Jenny. He had no idea how the events had transpired but he wanted blood from somebody. He walked around Jimmy clenching his fists and cursing him until Bobby came over and put his arm around him.

"Adam is okay," said Bobby. "He's with Doc, let's go see him, we'll deal with this later. The two of them walked down the side of the hill back toward the table where the skeletons sat.

Adam came running at full tilt and jumped into Jake's arms. Jake hugged him like he never hugged anyone in his life and the two just looked at each other.

"You got a lot to tell me," said Jake.

"I sure do and you aren't going to believe it. How is mom?"

"She is worried to death and as soon as I can, we're going to call her."

"Bobby, why don't you go with Adam and let him take you to the pontoon boat so you can see if there is anything interesting down there?" asked Jake.

"Will do," said Bobby and he put his hand on Adam's shoulder and they walked off.

"Bobby," said Jake. Bobby turned to look at him. "No more spook stories." Bobby chuckled then he beamed in the fact that they had Adam back.

"Okay Doc, what now?"

"Well, I think we need to tend to the wounded guy," said Doc. Doc was looking around the camp for something as he talked. He bent over and picked up a thin board about three feet long. Doc grabbed one end of a wooden bench and Jake got the other end and they headed up the side of the hill. When they reached Jimmy they turned it on its side and placed it next to him. They both took hold of Jimmy, doc was at his head and he held traction on it as they rolled him on his side with his back against the bench. They tied him on to it with scraps of cloth and bits of rope. They secured his head with a roll of ancient duct tape that was found in a box next to the table. Once they were satisfied he was secure the turned the bench back upright and carried Jimmy back down under the tarp. Once they were there they repeated the process but this time left Jimmy face down. Doc picked up the board he found earlier and shoved it down Jimmy pants until it stopped. The other end protruded above his head. The men tied straps around the board and Jimmy from his waist to his neck. They were tight. They stood him up and moved him to the chair that Adam had occupied for many hours across from the skeleton. Jimmy's eyes moved back and forth. Large beads of sweat popped up on his head and he was having problems maintaining his temperature with the injury he sustained. His bowels had let go and his pants were saturated with feces and urine. He was a pitiful sight.

"Now, I don't know who you are or why you are here. I don't even know why you had my nephew out here with you. It looks like you came here to dig up this burial and haul off what you found. That's a very bad thing to do. I mean, look at this poor fellow sitting across from you. He's been out here for eight hundred or a thousand years in peace then you come along." Jimmy's eyes cut back and forth. "I was going to kill you for taking the kid but it looks like you have done it yourself. Too bad it's going to take such a long time."

Jimmy had tears running down both cheeks when Adam and Bobby came back into the camp. Adam just glanced at Jimmy and walked by him. Bobby looked at him and didn't say anything. He knew the extent of the injury Jimmy had sustained but none of them let on to Adam just how bad it was or what would happen to Jimmy.

"Doc, Jake, they have the boat stuffed with everything from skeletons to ceramics. They were headed to sell it off somewhere," said Bobby.

"I've got an idea," said Jake. "We're going to take what's in the boat and get it in safe keeping."

"Safekeeping? What the hell you planning to do?" asked Doc.

"Trust me on this one," said Jake. Jake took out his cell phone and marked GPS coordinates and put it back in his pocket.

Chapter 18

Bobby headed back to his boat by himself. Adam took Doc and Jake to where the pontoon boat was tied. When they arrived at the boat neither Doc of Jake could believe what they were seeing. The size of the rig was impressive enough but the way it was rigged really got their attention.

"This guy was his own expeditionary force," wouldn't you say?" asked Doc.

"He could stay out forever on this thing as long as he had food and water and plenty of fuel to get back on. There's no telling where this boat has been," said Jake.

Doc stepped up on the deck of the boat and went back to the console. He turned the key and the motor started right up. He shut it down again and started looking around. Jake already had the tops off of many of the tubs and was repulsed by the contents.

"These were people," said Jake.

"What are we going to do with them? We can't' take them back up to the site. We wouldn't know what to do with them or where they came from," said Doc.

"We can't take them back up there for lots of reasons," said Jake recalling to himself some of the stories his grandmother Alene had told him about burying the dead.

Bobby motored the jon boat up next to the pontoon and hopped out of it and tied it off.

"Ahoy," said Jake with a smile.

"What's next?" asked Bobby.

"Doc and I were just talking about that. We need to get a move on. We're going to take both boats back to the landing. We're going to off load this cargo into our vehicles, then I'm going to make a few phone calls," said Jake.

Doc took the controls of the pontoon while Jake untied it. Jake and Adam rode with Bobby. Adam refused to get back on the pontoon boat. Soon both boats were heading south upstream toward the landing. Doc slipped the big boat in next to the dock on the end. One side of the boat was next to the land where a truck cold be parked and the other side was tied to the dock. People cold work on both sides. Once secure Bobby moved his truck down next to the boat and Doc started handing up tubs and boxes. Adam went up to Jake's truck and stretched out and went to sleep. Once Bobby's truck was full, Jake backed his truck down and the men finished the task. Doc started the pontoon back up and headed downstream again with Bobby behind him but this time at a much faster pace. They returned to the site and tied the boat out and left one last time for the boat landing.

"Okay, let's go back to where we came from. Or at least head in that general direction," said Jake. He and Adam pulled out of the boat landing area and headed west with Jake and Bobby close behind. It took about twenty five minutes before Jake could call Doc on the phone. When he did reach him they made a plan to pull off the road at the first safe place.

Doc pulled off to the right at a small country store and Bobby followed him. He pulled alongside of him and all of the men got out.

"Okay gentlemen, are you ready for

this?" asked Jake while holding his phone up.

He dialed the phone and Jenny answered it before it finished ringing the first time. Jake held the phone away from his ear as the barrage of language poured through the earpiece. Bobby and Doc looked on and smiled.

"Baby, I have Adam. He is fine. I couldn't call. Let me get Adam so he can say hello. Bobby is right here beside me," said Jake who was trying to keep up with the questions. Bobby overheard him and turned and walked into the store because he didn't quite feel up to a question and answer session.

"Momma," came the voice over the phone and Jenny started crying. "I'm okay, how are you? How is Sport?"

"We're fine now, I missed you so bad. I am happy you are okay," said Jenny to her son.

"Momma, you won't believe what happened, I can't wait to tell you. Oh, be sure to tell Sport that he got him right between the eyes," said Adam.

"What? What do you mean?" asked Jenny.

"Just let him know, he'll know what I'm talking about," said Adam. "Okay, we're going to go now. We will see you real soon."

When everyone was back in the vehicles, Jake walked back in the store and handed the clerk a tightly folded piece of paper with the GPS coordinates of the site written on it in pencil. "I want you to wait thirty minutes then open this up and dial 911. Read what it says on the paper and hang up. No need to tell them who gave it to you," he said and he turned and walked out.

They drove west until they hit the Florida Turnpike. They went through the toll booth and picked up a ticket for the north bound lane. They drove for about forty five minutes and pulled over at a service plaza. Adam got a hamburger and a soft drink, the men went to the bathroom and had some coffee. Jake called Jenny once again.

"We're gonna' be a little delayed coming home," he said. Jenny was upset because she wanted so desperately to see him and Adam after the harrowing couple of days.

"I don't understand," said Jenny. "Why don't you tell me where you are going to be and I'll just drive on up and meet you," she said.

"I've got some business to take care of and some things to set right," said Jake. "I should be home tomorrow night. I will call you, I promise."

"I guess, I don't understand but I suppose you have your reasons," she said. Jake told her he loved her and hung up. The group headed north on the turnpike. They eventually picked up 75 and kept going. When Jake hit Paine's Prairie he made another phone call. This time to an old friend. Not really expecting anyone on the other end to pick up the phone, the man he was calling answered. It was Ben Harker on the other end.

"Jake, how the heck are you. It's been a while," said Ben.

"Two...I need to get together with you this afternoon," said Jake. Jake nicknamed his former teacher from Haskell 'Two Feathers' because for as long as Jake knew him he wore two small beaded fathers in his long gray braided pony tail. Jake even tried the look while he was in Kansas but he just couldn't get used to it. Somehow if fit Ben perfectly. Even when lecturing in Washington or out on the golf course it made a remarkable statement that there was plenty of heart left in him to go toe to toe with the most fearsome opponent. Ben was a hard assed attorney with the Bureau of Indian Affairs who began a stint at the local university as a visiting scholar 6 years ago and never left. Prior to the BIA, right after he graduated from Harvard Law School, he ran with the American Indian Movement where he gained valuable experience defending a very small minority against goliath issue. In between he taught.

"Two…I need to come by your house and drop off some things," said Jake.

"What kind of things?" asked Ben.

"I don't really have time to explain right now but there is a major village site that got ransacked up on the St. Johns. Lots of players," said Jake.

"I'm not in town now but you can go by the house. The garage is open. There is a spare remote under the flower pot on the deck. If it's small enough you can just put it in the mailbox. Did you say St Johns River? I know who it is. He's in prison not too far from Gainesville," said Ben.

"Ben…I have two pickup loads of material. I will leave it in the garage," said Jake.

"What the hell happened?" asked Ben.

"I'll explain later. I want you to take care of it. I know that you are the only one that can

213

see to it that there will be no fighting with the state or anybody else over this. It's a big deal. Repatriations, lots of things to think about. Call me when you get back to town," said Jake and he hung up.

The two trucks eventually made into a quiet neighborhood on the outskirts of Gainesville. They made several turns and many stops and finally pulled in to Two's driveway. He lived in a spacious two story wooden house that was built in the late 1920's. The garage was added sometime in the 1960's and it looked like the rest of the house. Two bought it after he decided to take a full time faculty position at the university.

Jake backed up to the garage while Bobby maneuvered his truck out of the driveway so he could back in beside Jake. Jake got out and found the garage door controller and he opened the door. They spent the next forty minutes unloading the trucks. When they were done, Jake closed the door and they talked for a little while.

"Bobby, our work here is done. I want you to take Adam and head on back to the ranch, I got one more thing to do while I am in town," said Jake.

"What am supposed to tell Jenny when I come rolling up and you aren't with us?"

"Just tell her about what happened to us and that I am okay. Let her know that Doc is with me and we'll be back sometime tomorrow. Tell her to call me when you get there, I'll explain."

"Okay, you guys be careful," said Bobby as he was backing out of the driveway.

"Bye Jake! Bye Uncle Doc! See you tomorrow!" said Adam. He waved to them out of the back window until Bobby turned and the truck was out of sight.

Chapter 19

The first helicopter arrived at the site on the St. Johns River an hour before Jake made it to Two's house. Another hour went by before the air rescue chopper touched down. The paramedics tended to Jimmy Goodland the best they could. They didn't know for sure what had happened to him. They started and I.V., stabilized his spine, put him in a neck brace and got him onto the gurney where they put him under a warming blanket. He breathed fitfully under the oxygen mask. He couldn't cough because of his injury. He gurgled when he exhaled. The lead paramedic was on the phone with the doctor at the emergency room where they intended on delivering him. Jimmy lingered for a month before he expired from pneumonia alone in a respiratory ICU. No one knew who he was for 2 weeks before his death. He simply languished as J. Doe, disaster patient. Hospital officials were unsuccessful in all of their attempts to locate his wife who was still in Georgia when he died.

The paramedics on the scene had walked around the skeletons sitting across from Jimmy like it didn't exist. They never even questioned the bizarre scene. They were rightly concerned with their live patient and besides, that's what law enforcement was there for.

The cops took lots of pictures but really couldn't make much sense of anything. They saw the remnants of a camp, some equipment, a skeleton, pottery shards, junk and other things they couldn't identify. Eventually the entire scene was crawling with officers from a half dozen agencies. One astute game warden notified the BIA and several local museums. By the next morning a boat load of representatives from the American Indian Movement had arrived with a thousand yards of neon yellow crime scene tape, several tents, coolers full of food, communications gear and their own television crew. They staked out the entire complex and read from a laundry list of laws, case histories, and other examples of why they had the imminent right to control the site and anything happening on it for as long as they wanted to. The officials were baffled and once they concluded their investigation most of them left. Over the next several days several reporters from several of the state's largest newspapers ventured out to the site to try and make sense of the ensuing mayhem.

Jake called Two one more time and they talked about the man in prison. Two told Jake his name. Jake and Doc spent the night in the back of the truck just outside the gates of the Raiford Correctional Institute. When visiting hours started Doc dropped Jake off in front of the entrance and left for town. Jake walked in and emptied his pockets in front of two fat guards who looked like they were still suffering the untoward effect of a big night out on the town. Jake identified himself twice and let them know who he was there to visit.

"Hey, are you in Indian?" asked the younger of the two. Jake just looked at him and didn't answer.

"Think we ought to search him?" he asked the other guard.

"For what?"

"I don't know. Maybe he has a pistol in his ass or something," said the guard snickering.

"Shut up, let him through," said the older guard.

Jake went through the metal detector without incident and was led down a long brightly lit corridor to a steel door. The guard punched a few numbers into a key pad then turned the oversized steel handle. The door opened to a row of cheap plastic chairs each tucked into an individual cubby with sound absorbing sides. Thick glass with wires crisscrossed inside of it separated the cubby from the other side where the prisoners were. Jake sat down and looked through the window. A few minutes later a skinny whiskered man was led to the seat in front of Jake. The guard sat him down and took a couple of steps back and just stood there as if his presence would prevent some sort of all out prison riot. The man sat down and looked back at Jake.

Jake picked up the phone as did the man on the other side.

"I found the site," said Jake. The man on the other side had an astounded look on his face.

"How"?

"You wouldn't believe it if I told you," said Jake.

"Try me."

"I can't, don't have time. I know what you were trying to do though," said Jake.

"What's your point?" asked the man.

"You don't have much longer in here," said Jake.

"Listen, the whole thing was a put up," said the man.

"I know," said Jake.

"I got the shit end of a very bad deal. I was going to jail no matter what. Judge couldn't pin anything on me so in a series of court appearances he found me in contempt. They had me in jail in Sable County for nearly a year before they realized they could send me here. I suppose I was in contempt in the strict legal sense. All I know is that he had to stash me somewhere after they found my wife dead. That's another story," the man said.

"I know the story," said Jake. "I also know that you were fighting for your life and for the site."

"You do?"

"Yep. You're going to get out soon. The site will be taken care of. There are people there now that will ensure that. The stuff that you removed will be put back where it is supposed to be. I need to know the others that you sold to. I promise no one will ever know anything. Call me when you get out," said Jake.

"I had my back against the wall. I lost everything including my job," said the man.

"You're going to be okay," said Jake. "Here is my phone number."

"Okay," said the man.

Jake got up from his chair to leave and turned around.

"Do you still have a GPS?" he asked the man.

"Got a couple of them back home," he said.

"Okay, good. Don't forget to call me," said Jake and he turned and walked out.

Jake walked out into the stunning daylight in front of the prison. He called Doc to pick him up. It took Doc nearly an hour to get back to the jail. When Doc arrived Jake got in the truck and they left to finally go home.

"I got one more stop," said Jake.

"What now? Can't we just be done and go home?" asked Doc.

"Nothing much, just need to make a stop to help a friend out."

"Lead the way my friend," said Doc. "As long as it is south of here I will take you anywhere."

Eventually the pair pulled off the interstate and headed for Micanopy. They took a couple of dirt roads and ended up deep in the woods near Orange Lake. It was spot that Jake's grandfather had taken him to on several occasions.

"Stop here," said Jake. He got out of the truck and went to the back of it and took out a coffee can and a folding shovel.

"What the heck are you doing?" asked Doc.

"Leaving something for an old friend," he said.

He told Doc to sit tight and he made his way out into the woods. Once he felt like the spot was obscure enough he dug a hole and sat the coffee can with over a pound of Spanish gold in it and most of the twenty thousand dollar deposit Jimmy had collected from the men in Tampa. He sat the can down in the hole and covered it back over. In a few months the imprisoned archaeologist would be freed and a lot of other more deserving people would be headed for jail if he decided to contact Jake. This wouldn't help him get his life back completely but it would certainly help ease the sting of what happened to him. Jake took four separate GPS readings and wrote them all down. He also took several photos with his phone and he left.

Jake emerged from the woods and got in the truck. He looked at Doc and said, "Points south, let's go home."

"I am with you on that, "said Doc.

The End

Epilogue

Three days after the discovery of the site by government officials the entire place was abuzz with equipment, people, reporters, and local onlookers. The people from AIM kept the locals off the site as best they could but they never missed the chance to explain their cause to them either. On the morning of the third day, contractors form the state in conjunction with AIM, the Native Graves Protection group from Washington, D.C, local clergy, spiritualists, and at least one small group of stoned new age priests gather at the top of the site. The hippies took over one area and burned bundles of aromatic herbs and waved the smoke around themselves with a turkey vulture feather that one of them had found near the water next to a rotting garfish carcass. The leader had assigned some sort of spiritual significance to the feather than only his group of followers understood. The AIM people were more solemn and didn't communicate with anyone else and would have been happy if everyone else had left them to take care of the rites themselves. When the signal was given, several camera flashes went off and a small bull dozer went to work pushing the spoils of the dig back into the trench from where it first came. Junior the 'arkeelogist' and his sidekick Hole were sealed over with a hundred tons of backfill courtesy of the State of Florida. In less than thirty minutes they were buried along with the skeletal remains they had found. Perhaps in a thousand years, someone would dig them up.

Six months later a store in Soho was raided by agents from the Department of the

Interior. In addition to the remains of several endangered species, they recovered two intact skeletons that later proved to be from Florida. Later that day the four inch thick mahogany door on Rudy Rodriquez' house came crashing in as he was getting ready for a dinner party with some of Miami's most noted art crowd. Agents removed four trunks full of pottery and human remains.

The archaeologist who blew the whistle cashed in his coffee can for nearly a quarter of a million dollars. He remarried and took a job in Mexico City where he teaches in one of the local universities.

Two worked for ten years cataloging the material that Jake and Doc recovered from the pontoon boat. Each item was cast for replicas. When the last piece was done, he invited Jake and Doc back out to the site for the repatriation of the original pieces.